# Red Thread
# Sisters

CAROL ANTOINETTE PEACOCK

SCHOLASTIC INC.

ISBN 978-0-545-62622-4

12 11 10 9 8 7 6 5 4 3 2                    13 14 15 16 17 18/0

Printed in the U.S.A.                                    40

First Scholastic printing, September 2013

Set in Weiss Std
Book design by Kate Renner

For children in orphanages
all over the world
waiting for families of their own

An invisible red thread connects those who are destined to meet, regardless of time, place, or circumstance. The thread may stretch or tangle, but it will never break.

—ANCIENT CHINESE LEGEND

# one

"Shu Ling, where are you?" Zhang Wen called. Chilled in the early morning air of September, Wen pulled a thin sweater around her shoulders. The orphanage threw a long shadow across the courtyard.

*Where is she?* Wen wondered. *Today of all days!*

Wen's new sandals pinched her toes as she picked her way through the bits of glass and metal strewn along the path. Dingy diapers were spread on the bushes to dry. From the open windows of the orphanage, she heard the babies crying.

"Shu Ling, please! Where are you?"

Wen knew she couldn't have gone far, not with her bad leg.

Wen stepped over some rusted pipes and then, striding through a thick patch of long grasses, she veered left until she reached the hill ahead. There she saw her friend, crouched like a cricket on a stack of tires. Her bony knees pointed upward, her elbows jutted from her sides.

"Finally!" Wen said. "I've been looking everywhere for you."

"I'm here," said Shu Ling. Her voice was low. "Our place."

She swept her arm across the dusty space, surrounded by a gully filled with trash.

"Of course this is where you'd be." Wen wrung her skirt as if to squeeze out the sadness rising inside her like a flood.

"You have new clothes." Shu Ling appraised her.

Wen hoisted up the denim skirt that Auntie Lan Lan had laid out for her that morning. "The skirt's just newer than usual, that's all. It's a little big." She combed her fingers through her short hair, so the black clumps on top would lie flat.

"You look good." Shu Ling rose from the tires, teetered, and then rested her arm on Wen.

Wen felt the familiar weight of Shu Ling's arm, fitting as perfectly as a puzzle piece in the hollow of her shoulder. *Say it*, she told herself. *Just say it.*

Wen cleared her throat. *"Zai jian,"* she said. "Good-bye. I have to go now."

"Your new family? They're all here?" Shu Ling swayed. "Just like the photo?"

Wen nodded. "Like the photo."

The snapshot of Wen's new family had come a month ago, all the way from America. The day the photo arrived, Wen and Shu Ling sat on the cement floor of the common room, the family portrait between them. They admired Wen's mother, her frizzy hair the color of corn and funny little eyeglasses perched on her nose. Beside the mother stood a stout father with a bald head.

"Round Man," Wen had named him, and Shu Ling laughed. On his back, Round Man carried a grinning, pigtailed Chinese girl, who must also have been adopted. Taped to the photo was a note, written in neat Chinese characters:

> Dear Zhang Wen,
>
> Here is a photo of us, your new family. We live in a town near a city called Boston in the state of Massachusetts. We have been waiting for you for a long time. Your new room is all ready. You will go to school with Emily on the school bus. We can't wait to meet you and welcome you into our family.
>
> See you soon,
>
> Christine McGuire (your mom)
> Richard McGuire (your dad)
> Emily McGuire (your sister, seven years old, favorite color pink)

After they had read the note, Wen flipped back to the glossy picture, because words made her leaving too real. "Your mom and your dad and your sister named Emily," Shu Ling said, as if she were chanting. Then her voice wobbled. After that, Wen hid the photograph under her straw mattress so Shu Ling wouldn't have to see Wen's family when she didn't have a family of her own yet.

Now Wen reached up and brushed a lock of hair from Shu Ling's eyes. "Remember our deal. Whoever got picked first would get a family for the other. Once I'm in America, I'll find a family for you! And then we can visit each other, Shu Ling. All the time."

"But how can we be sure, Wen?"

"I wouldn't leave if I didn't know you'd be coming too."

"Director Feng says I'm unadoptable." Darkness like the sky before a spring dust storm crossed Shu Ling's face. "He says I'm getting too old, and besides—"

Both girls glanced at Shu Ling's misshapen right leg, shorter than the other, her foot twisted inward.

"I'll find you a family," Wen said. "Before my twelfth birthday in April. You'll come right after me! In less than a year, Shu Ling!"

Shu Ling stared at the cabbage from the previous night's dinner, now rotting at the bottom of the ditch. She was silent.

Gently, Wen drew Shu Ling toward her. "In the meantime, while I'm finding you a family over there, be sure to be very good. Otherwise, Director Feng won't put you on the list for adoption. Remember that, Shu Ling. Don't lie too long in your cot in the morning, OK? I won't be here to wake you."

"I'll get up," Shu Ling said.

"Be sure to help with all the feedings. And don't go cud-
dling your favorite babies extra. Not until you've given a
bottle to every baby in every crib."

"I can do the feedings fine. You know that."

"Also," Wen went on, "do all the chores the aunties tell
you. Don't forget the bleach when you wash the walls. And
don't sneak off to our hill to draw. Your pictures are so
good, Shu Ling. But they'll get you in trouble."

"Wen, you worry too much." Shu Ling took both of
Wen's hands into her own. "I'll be OK."

"I'll think of you every day," Wen said.

"You'll be so far away." Bending down, Shu Ling pressed
her cheek against Wen's new sweater and embraced her.

"Zhang Wen," a voice called. "Your family is here! Come
now!"

Wen's heart raced. "That's Director Feng. I should go.
*Zai jian*, Shu Ling."

Wen felt Shu Ling's grasp tighten. Then she heard
Director Feng shout louder. "Zhang Wen, do not keep
your new family waiting!"

"Shu Ling," Wen said, "I have to go."

Shu Ling clung to Wen, glued to Wen's body.

Very slowly, Wen took Shu Ling's hands, knuckles white
with gripping. One by one, Wen pried each finger from
her shoulder and released herself.

"*Zai jian*," Wen said.

"*Zai jian*." Shu Ling stroked Wen's cheek. Then she

slipped a rolled-up paper in Wen's skirt pocket. "For later."

"*Xie xie*, thank you." Wen tucked the piece of paper deeper into her pocket. "Now remember, I'll get you a family as soon as I can." She traced Shu Ling's face with her fingertips. "We'll see each other again."

"You promise?" asked Shu Ling.

"I promise," Wen answered.

Then she turned and ran toward the orphanage to meet her new family.

# two

"Hurry, they're here!" Auntie Lan Lan, the auntie in charge of the older kids, stood at the back door, just off the infant room. Behind her, bamboo cribs were crammed so close, their railings touched.

"Tears on your happiest day, Wen? What will your new family think?" Auntie Lan Lan took a tissue from the pocket of her white auntie's coat and dabbed Wen's eyes. "That's better. Such a big journey ahead for such a small girl! Let's go!" Auntie Lan Lan grabbed Wen's hand. "They're in Director Feng's office."

Wen could hardly believe this was really happening to her. She had always been the one who just observed adoptions, like a bystander at somebody else's festival. She'd seen baby Ying Ying, padded with layers of quilted jackets, cling to her new mother the minute she held her. She'd watched four-year-old Jun Ren, who'd come to the orphanage with weakened lungs, sprint on skinny legs toward his new parents. Once, when the aunties were very busy, Wen had shampooed Hong's hair, helped her with her leggings and her ruffled jacket, then placed her on her mother's lap.

"Hello, my new mother," Hong practically sang. As she saw the other kids get new families, Wen felt a longing even deeper than her hunger at the evening meal, when breakfast had been so long ago.

Now, at last, it was her turn. She was on her way to meet her new mama and a family of her own. Wen gripped Auntie Lan Lan's hand as they approached Director Feng's office.

"Hurry, we're late." Auntie Lan Lan pulled Wen's arm.

Dazed, Wen heard Auntie Lan Lan's voice fade in and out, like the TV with the broken volume button.

Wen saw Director Feng's office door ajar. She took a deep breath and felt Auntie Lan Lan's hands on the small of her back, pushing her forward, into the office.

"Come in," said Director Feng tersely. "You have kept—"

But Wen stopped listening. She had turned to stone. She knew that her new family was right there, but she couldn't move. Unable to raise her head, she studied the thick black scrapes across the worn tile floor. She wasn't supposed to be this afraid, not on the happiest day of her life.

Who were these people? How could they be her family? They were strangers. Except for the worn photo under her mattress, Wen didn't know them at all.

Wen felt their eyes fixed on her. What did they see as they gazed at her? Were her clumps of hair lying flat? Did she look like she'd be no trouble? What if they changed their minds and didn't want her after all?

Then, through lowered lashes, Wen took her first glimpse of her new family. The mother and father and little sister named Emily were lined up like kids in a row, waiting for the aunties to count them at bedtime.

Wen took another peek. The mother's hair was yellower than she'd expected, her skin was paler, and she had more wrinkles around her mouth than in the snapshot. Her eyes were very round and very blue. Wen had never seen such eyes before.

The father wasn't all that fat. His bald head was shiny, as if it had been polished. The little Chinese kid, who had to be Emily, had fuller cheeks than any of the little girls in the orphanage, and her hair was glossier.

All of a sudden, Emily tore across the room and flung her arms around Wen's waist.

*"Wen-nie!"* She spit out a stream of English words that washed over Wen like dishwater poured out after kitchen chores.

Then Wen smelled the fragrance of lemon. Raising her head, she saw the woman with the sunshine hair, right beside her. Her new mother moved nearer, ready to hug her.

Wen stiffened. Without warning, she knew she didn't want this foreign lady to touch her. She made herself sink, momentarily, into her new mother's embrace, then pulled away.

When her father came toward her, Wen stepped back.

Not another hug, so soon. Her father extended his hand toward her and timidly, she took his fingers. "*Ni hao*, Wen." Her new father grinned at her so broadly his eyes twinkled.

Wen tried to remember one of the English phrases Auntie Lan Lan had taught her especially for this day. But her mind was blank.

From behind her, Wen heard Auntie Lan Lan whisper, "I-am-so-glad . . ."

"I-am-so-glad-to-meet-you," said Wen.

"*Wo de nu er*," said her mother, in poorly pronounced Chinese. "My daughter."

Wen shuddered. Hearing her mother speak flattened Chinese made her seem even stranger.

Then Wen heard her mother talk and Auntie Lan Lan translate her words for Director Feng, who spoke no English. "Mrs. McGuire will leave the blankets and orphanage donation check here. The family will give Wen the small gifts so she can leave them for the other children before she goes. I will take the candies to distribute later. Then the McGuires will wait for Wen by the jeep."

Wen's mother presented Auntie Lan Lan with a box of M&M packets and, smiling, handed Wen a large green plastic bag. Wen peeked again at her mother. Her hair was almost as yellow as the yellow crayon in the small-children's activity room.

"Be quick! Do not keep your new family waiting again," said Director Feng.

Her feet limber at last, Wen rushed from the room. "Auntie Lan Lan, I want to put the little presents on the beds." What could she find in that bag that would be special for Shu Ling?

Nodding, Auntie Lan Lan hefted the box with the candies to her chest. "Ah, M&M's! The Americans always bring M&M's. The children will go crazy. Aunties, too!"

Wen hurried to the bedroom where all the girls slept. The twelve metal cots squeezed together left little space for aisles. Wen dumped out yo-yos, beaded hair clips, and Disney key chains on Shu Ling's bed. She sorted through the trinkets until she found a set of slender drawing pencils, all the colors of the rainbow, and a small pad of paper. Wen hid the pencils and paper under Shu Ling's pillow.

As the tightness in her chest eased a little, Wen sighed. Now Shu Ling would have something to remember her by. She'd make her sketches better than ever. Wen grazed her fingertips across the top of Shu Ling's bed.

She'd first met Shu Ling when she was sitting on this same cot, six years ago. The aunties had found Wen at the gate and brought her here, where she huddled, all alone. She couldn't stop shivering. Suddenly she heard a *stomp-drag, stomp-drag* and raised her eyes. A tall girl with a long braid down her back appeared at the door and limped toward her, carrying a bowl of steaming soup. Very carefully, the girl put the hot bowl in Wen's hands. Then she covered her legs with a blanket and patted her arm. "Don't worry. My name is Shu Ling. I'm your friend," she'd said. She helped Wen lift the hot soup to her lips. Wen drank. "I'm in the next bed over," Shu Ling had said. "You'll sleep right here, by me." And from that night on, she did.

Now Wen wove through the rows of cots and went to the small, cracked window, propped open with a stick. Leaning far to the left, she could just see the dusty space. Was Shu Ling still there, waiting on the stack of tires?

But the tires were just tires and the hill was empty.

Wen felt an ache come so hard she doubled over, as if she'd been punched in the belly. *Not now*, she told herself. There was no time to be sad. She had to go.

She put the paper Shu Ling had given her into her new backpack, along with an Olympics sweatshirt, some smooth pebbles she and Shu Ling had collected, and her family portrait from under her mattress. With one final glance at the bedroom, she flung her backpack over her shoulder and started down the dark hall. Wen looked into the boys' bedroom, its seven cots jammed tight, a lightbulb dangling from a wire overhead. Next, she passed the infant room, where twenty black-haired babies lay, head to toe, two or three in a crib. Across the way, in the small-children's activity room, Wen saw the toddlers, slouching in rusty walkers. At last, Wen reached the orphanage foyer.

"Good-bye, Wen." At the open door, Auntie Lan Lan

clutched a tissue, as if she'd been wiping her own eyes.

"I'm scared, Auntie Lan Lan." Wen peered out the door at her new family clustered around the jeep, waiting for her.

Auntie Lan Lan knelt and put her face close to Wen's. "Try not to be scared. It will take time. But they're a nice family, these people, I can tell." Then she went on. "Have I told you the ancient Chinese legend, Wen, the one about the red thread?"

Wen shook her head.

Auntie Lan Lan spoke softly. "It's a very old story that goes like this: There is an invisible red thread that connects those who are destined to meet. No matter what place or circumstance, the red thread may stretch or tangle, but it will never break." She paused. "This thread has brought you and your family together. At this orphanage, on this day. You and the McGuires are meant to be. Believe this, Wen. The red thread connects you." Auntie Lan Lan clasped both her hands over Wen's. "You'll grow up so strong and smart in America. Remember, be a very good girl."

"I will." Wen grasped Auntie Lan Lan's hands.

"It's time, Wen, they're waiting for you," she said.

Wen let go of Auntie Lan Lan and walked toward her new family.

A driver in a black uniform stood by the jeep's doors. "Wennie!" called Emily, patting the place beside her. Wen wedged into the backseat beside Emily and her mother. Her father sat up front, next to the driver, who started up the engine.

The jeep approached the orphanage gate. Over the gate stretched a wide arch of worn tiles. Hammered iron characters, some bleeding rust onto the tiles, announced the place: TONG DU CHILDREN'S WELFARE INSTITUTE.

This was the gate where Wen's mother had left her, the winter she was five. Her mother had just had a baby boy. On a very cold day, she'd swung a big sack of dry noodles onto her back and called for Wen. Wen's mother took her hand and told her they were going for a walk. Her toes cramped in her cotton shoes, Wen's feet began to hurt as they journeyed along winding roads. Finally, she and her mother reached a hill where a crumbling pink building stood.

Wordless, they approached the building. Wen's mother stopped and propped her sack of dry noodles against the gate. She motioned for Wen to sit against the noodles and pinned a scrap of paper onto her jacket. Then her mother began to cry. Wen heard her choking through her sobs, as if she were trying to explain something to her. But Wen's mother's words were garbled and Wen didn't understand.

Then Wen's mother grew still and told Wen she was a good girl. "I love you, Wen," she said.

"I love you too, Mama," Wen replied.

Wen's mother stooped to kiss Wen's cheek. She hugged her for a long time before she let go. Then, with a final look over her shoulder, her mother went away.

"Mama!" Wen called, more scared than she'd ever been in her life. But her mother did not return. The sun went down and the trees around the building towered over her like dragons. The hard noodles pressed against her back. She got up to search for her mother, but the night was so dark, she couldn't see in front of her. She sat back down by the gate.

"I love you," Wen called to the darkness.

There was only silence.

"Mama!" Wen wept. "I love you."

But still there was only silence. No reply came.

All night long Wen waited. In the morning, a lady in a short white coat found her and called out, "Another gate child!"

The woman brought her inside and tried to give her hot tea but Wen scrambled back to the gate to wait for her mother. The white-coat lady scooped Wen from the ground and read the note pinned on Wen's jacket.

"No need to wait here at the gate, Zhang Wen," the woman said. "The drought has been too long and your family has gone. You live with us now."

That was a little over six years ago.

Now, at the gate, the jeep stopped. Wen held her hands tightly in her lap. Were they going back? Had they forgotten something? Or had her parents changed their minds already?

Abruptly, the jeep lurched forward. Wen looked back at the crumbling pink building set on the top of the hill. When the dust rose and blocked her view, Wen turned and stared straight ahead, the orphanage behind her.

# three

The jeep swerved down the rutted dirt road. Jostling in the backseat, Wen clung to the armrest. She had ridden in a car only three times before. Once when Wen had a rotting tooth, Auntie Bi Yu, the nurse-auntie, drove her to the dental clinic. Another time, the day Ying Ying got adopted, her new parents drove four of Ying Ying's friends, including Wen and Shu Ling, to the McDonald's in the city. Then, during the long drought last summer, she and some of the other kids had bounced in the back of the truck all the way to the village, where government officials were distributing buckets of water.

Now, as Wen peered out the jeep window, she waited for the joy of release. She had often daydreamed about what it would be like to leave Tong Du for good. As she scoured the bathroom walls or stirred the infants' corn-meal, she had imagined departing through the orphanage gate. She had planned to feel free, like the swallows soaring wherever they wanted over the courtyard trees.

Instead, Wen pulled her thighs to her chest and hid her face against her knees. This was the beginning of her new life, and all she could think about was Shu Ling waving good-bye, getting farther and farther away. Wen curled up even smaller, shutting her eyes tight to hold back her tears.

"*Hao ba*, Wen? OK?" Over the rumble of the jeep, Wen heard her mother's voice as she read from a ring of phrase cards Wen had seen other new parents use before. Each card had a Chinese word on one side, the English translation on the other. "Wen, *hao ba?*"

Wen nodded, keeping her chin down. Beside her, she felt her mother pat a clump of her hair. Covering her head with both arms, Wen slunk toward the floor, beyond her mother's reach.

After a bumpy, two-hour jeep ride, Wen and her family stopped at a big city called Taiyuan. That afternoon, they took an overnight train ride to Beijing. Wen had never ridden on a train. Like a long snake spitting smoke, the train swerved and hissed. Out the window of their sleeper compartment, Wen saw big fields, the wheat already cut and drying along the sides of the roads.

At bedtime, Wen lay on the top of the second bunk and listened to the whistle of the train as it sped through the night. When she finally fell asleep, Wen dreamed she was back at the orphanage, racing through the dark halls.

"Shu Ling, where are you?" she cried.

She checked the infant room, the kitchen, and then the small-children's activity room. But she didn't find Shu Ling. She strode up the hill, where she figured Shu Ling must be drawing in the dirt. But Shu Ling wasn't there. Wen tried to keep running but her feet turned heavy, like great stones, and she couldn't move. She collapsed on the hill, still calling for Shu Ling.

When she woke in the morning, Wen felt as paralyzed as she had in her bad dream, only worse, because she knew, for sure, that Shu Ling was really gone.

They got off the train in Beijing, where the McGuires stayed at a big hotel at least ten stories high. Wen marveled at the hotel's huge glass windows and moving stairs. Was this what the houses would be like in America?

The next afternoon, Wen and her family boarded a plane for America. Auntie Lan Lan had prepared Wen for planes. "Airplanes are like great big birds. They fly in the sky but they don't fall to the ground," Auntie Lan Lan had explained. "The plane will bring you to America, the land of opportunity. . . . Ah, Wen, America! There are such big houses there and a McDonald's on every corner."

On the plane, Wen sat beside her father, while her mother and Emily got the seats behind them. As they waited for the plane to take off, Wen's mother put her hand on Wen's arm and whispered, *"Bu yao jin.* It's nothing to worry about. *Bu yao jin."*

Wen tried not to wince at her mother's toneless Chinese. Instead, she studied her mother's pale skin and round eyes. If she looked at her mother long enough, maybe she would get used to her.

Beside her, her father got out the card ring and showed her a picture of a plane, the words "Airplane" and *"Fei ji"* on reverse sides of the card.

*"Fei ji.* OK." He thumped the airplane window and grinned at her. Her father talked too loudly, as if shouting would help her understand. Wen forced a small smile.

When the plane rose from the ground, Wen felt her stomach do a flip-flop. She was in the air! It was a good thing Auntie Lan Lan had told her about airplanes not falling from the sky. Wen blinked in disbelief as puffy white clouds floated right outside her window. She was up so high, she must be near the sun itself.

Later, when her father had dozed off, Wen slipped Shu Ling's roll of paper from her backpack and smoothed it on her lap.

With charcoal, Shu Ling had sketched the two of them, standing side by side. Their elbows linked, the girls wore their favorite clothes, assigned to them from the common wardrobe. Wen had on her sparkly pink sweatshirt and Shu Ling was in the flare jeans that hid her bad leg so nicely. Their smiles were as wide as the slices of watermelon the aunties served as a special treat in the summer.

Underneath the picture Shu Ling had written, "I will always remember you, *mei mei."*

*Mei mei.* Little sister.

Wen could almost hear Shu Ling's voice saying the words out loud for the first time. Wen was six years old when she and Shu Ling had been scrubbing the courtyard tiles. Shu Ling told Wen her story, how a policeman had discovered her, just three months old, in a melon crate, left on the steps of a hospital. Her parents had wrapped tape around her bad leg. Shu Ling said that her parents must not have wanted a broken baby, so they threw her away.

Shaking her head, Wen told Shu Ling that her parents hadn't just left her anywhere. They'd left Shu Ling at a hospital so the doctors could find her and fix her.

Shu Ling had straightened, as if a basin heavy with wet laundry had been lifted from her back. "So they weren't just throwing me away." Shu Ling thought for a long time. Then she thanked Wen for telling her this new thing.

When Wen stretched for the bucket to get back to work, Shu Ling had warned her to be very careful with the bleach. "No matter what happens, *mei mei*, from now on, we're family."

*Mei mei*. Now, the portrait on her lap, Wen read Shu Ling's words again. She told herself not to cry. If her new family knew she was sad, they might think she wasn't grateful and give her back. As soon as the plane landed in America, her mother and father and Emily might get up from their seats, say "Wait here," and then never return. And then what would happen to her?

Very carefully, Wen rolled up the scroll and put it into her backpack. Lulled by the drone of the plane, she finally slept. She woke as the plane jolted to a stop. Her father nudged Wen's arm and pointed out the window.

*Mei Guo!* America!

All she saw was a vast stretch of concrete, as big as a wheat field, with airplanes lined up in rows. This was America? Where were the big houses and the McDonald's on every corner?

*"Di er jia fei ji.* Plane number two," she heard her father say. Fighting her drowsiness, Wen tried to open her eyes wide to see more of this America. Her mother took her elbow and guided her to a long line of people waiting for a man to stamp their papers. Wen twisted the straps of her backpack. Why was it taking so long to get into America?

Finally, with her father and Emily right behind, Wen and her mother approached the desk. The man stamping papers stopped and took a long look at Wen. Wen felt his round eyes burrowing right through her. His eyes darted from her to her mother then back to her. He shook his head, like he was confused, like something was wrong. Wen covered her face with her hands.

"My daughter." Wen's mother placed her hand on Wen's shoulder.

Wen remembered her mother saying those same words when they first met at the orphanage.

Then Wen's mother said it again. "My daughter." Her raised voice sounded mad, like Auntie Lan Lan's when a kid spilled food at dinner or the boys started punching one another at bedtime.

Gently, Wen's mother reached for Wen's hands. Wen uncovered her face and stepped closer to her mother. As the line moved, Wen peeked at the mean man. He was stamping their papers quickly, his hands flying, his eyes directed straight down, as if he was scared her mother would yell again.

Wen wanted to thank her mother for making the man stop staring at her. But her mother didn't know much Chinese and Wen was so nervous, she couldn't remember any of the English she had thought she knew so well.

After the McGuires filed into the second plane, Wen slept through the whole flight. Once they landed, Wen's father led the family to a big wheel where they got their suitcases, then wove through the crowded airport to the street. Wen's mother herded them to a line that said T-A-X-I. Finally, Wen's father opened a door to a yellow car with wide leather seats.

"*Jia*," her mother said as she helped Wen buckle her seat belt. "Home."

# four

All Wen could see was darkness. She squinted out the window as big cars on the wide, lighted road streamed past them. Then their driver slowed down onto a curving ramp leading to smaller streets with leafy trees outlined against the black sky. Wen could make out rows of houses set behind neat squares of grass. The car stopped at a brick house with wide windows. Emily clambered out of the backseat, took Wen's hand, and led her up the walk.

"*Huan ying*, Wen. Welcome!" Wen's mother said as her father unlocked the front door.

Still holding Wen's hand, Emily brought her into the house. Wen gasped. The hallway was as big as a room! The ceiling hung high above her, as if it were a sky.

Emily led her to a room down the hall. She waved her arm from Wen to the room and back to Wen, making a big sweep through the air. "Wen's!" she exclaimed.

What was she talking about?

Emily pulled Wen into the room. "Wen's!" she repeated, planting both feet on the floor. Without warning, Emily flung herself down on the rug, her face toward the ceiling, her arms and legs spread toward the four walls. "Wen's!" she shouted, from the floor.

*This whole room, for me?* Wen thought she should reenter the room on her knees, as if she were visiting the sleeping place of an empress. The walls were painted deep purple and the bed was covered with a lavender quilt. Stuffed animals sat heaped along the pillow. All those stuffed animals—enough for almost every baby and little kid in the whole orphanage! And the books! So many books, lined up neatly in a bookcase, ready to be read. In the corner, Wen saw a small white desk and a chair. How could one room belong just to her?

Emily sat on the fluffy, purple bed. Then, crouching, she pulled out a second bed, nestled under the first. Emily raised two fingers. "Wen's . . . *trun-dle.*"

Wen's mother came into the room and said something to Emily, who nodded and replied. Wen tilted her head, trying to understand. Where had all her English gone? She felt as if some giant lock inside her brain had mysteriously clamped shut over all the English she'd ever known.

Wen had studied English even before she went to school. A month after she'd arrived at the orphanage, five-year-old Wen was helping in the small-children's activity room, where she discovered some English picture books. After dinner, she had pored over the tattered books, connecting the words to the illustrations. Her favorite story was about a lady who went to a dance but lost a glass shoe, which a prince used to find her so they could live happily ever after.

When she was eight, Teacher Jun began real English lessons. From old workbooks, Wen sounded out English words and learned to link them into sentences and repeat the lines out loud with the other students.

Eight months ago, Auntie Lan Lan had heard Wen was going to America. "Your English must be even better," she told Wen, and started giving her extra lessons every night.

"You must learn to make real sentences," Auntie Lan Lan had said. "It's not enough to just repeat what the teacher says."

While they fed the babies, Auntie Lan Lan had quizzed her. "Name?" Auntie Lan Lan drilled. "I am Wen," Wen would call. "Good. Season?" Auntie Lan Lan asked. "It is summer," Wen answered, as if they were tossing a ball back and forth.

And now all that English was trapped inside her, somewhere Wen couldn't find.

In the hallway, her father stretched and opened his mouth, making big yawns. When he caught Wen's eye, he began to pretend to snore, interspersed with long whistles. Then he grinned at Wen.

Beside him, her mother shook her head, making clucking noises, like she was laughing at him. She took the ring of cards from his pocket.

"*Shui?* Sleep?" She showed Wen a card and then rested her cheek on her hands, folded sideways like a pillow.

Wen's mother gestured toward the room across from Wen's. She ruffled Emily's hair. "Wen, *shui* with *mei mei?* Little sister?" her mother asked.

"Wennie, *shui* with *mei mei*," Emily begged.

Wen felt her mouth go dry. She couldn't call Emily *mei mei*, because her throat would shrivel and she would choke. She was the *mei mei*, not this little girl. The only person saying *mei mei* should be Shu Ling, declaring that no matter what, Wen was her little sister and they were family.

Emily grabbed Wen around the waist and tried to pull her across the hall.

Wen stood firm, still thinking of Shu Ling.

"Not *shui* with *mei mei?*" Wen's mother breathed deeply, as if she were holding back a sigh.

Freeing herself from Emily's grasp, Wen stood apart, unsure. Would they think she was ungrateful if she didn't sleep with Emily? With slow, shaky steps, Wen walked into her new room and sat on her own bed. She waited for her mother and Emily to yell at her.

But neither one shouted. In the hallway, Wen saw Emily's lip quiver. Her mother said something to her in soothing tones, and then came into Wen's room. "*Shui zhe li?* Sleep here?" Wen's mother tapped her bed.

Wen nodded, then put her face in her hands.

At the orphanage, when Wen or Shu Ling had been

caught by one of the aunties for talking late at night or for not scouring the dinner pots shiny enough, they covered their faces with their hands while an auntie yelled. The other kids did it too. If you covered your face, you hid your shame at doing something very bad.

Wen felt her mother's fingers gently lift her hands from her face.

"*Bu yao jin*. It's nothing to worry about," her mother said softly. "*Bu yao jin*," she repeated, as if she knew the words by heart. When Wen uncovered her face, her mother was smiling at her. Then she handed Wen a pair of fluffy blue gathered pants and a matching top. "PJs."

Wen wondered why her mother was saying single alphabet letters. She put the pants and the top down and then climbed into her bed, still wearing her denim skirt and sweater she'd worn when she'd last seen Shu Ling.

"*Wan an*, Wen," her mother said. "Good night."

Wen saw her mother coming nearer, as if to kiss her. Her mother's frizzy blonde hair came so close, Wen could see each separate curl.

The aunties had never kissed her or any of the other kids. The last person to kiss Wen was her first mother. She had pulled Wen toward her and told Wen she was a good girl. Then she'd kissed Wen on the cheek and gone away.

Fear, like the flames from a grease fire in a pan, ripped

through Wen's body. As her new mother bent closer, Wen turned her head the other way.

She heard her mother sigh, then pat the pillow near Wen's hair as she got up to leave.

As soon as she was sure her mother wasn't coming back, Wen sank into her soft bed, the sheets as fragrant as the peonies that grew behind the orphanage. When she rolled over, no wires poked her back. No smell of musky hay filled her nostrils. Instinctively, Wen reached for Shu Ling's cot.

At the orphanage, as soon as the aunties left, Wen and Shu Ling would push their cots together so they could talk during the night. Only Shu Ling knew that Wen was afraid of the dark. Sometimes, when Wen heard rats scampering under the beds, she clung to Shu Ling. Worse than the dark were the rats! Whispering in Wen's ear, Shu Ling recited the nursery rhymes she'd learned at the orphanage when she was little. Shu Ling wove together verses about kites and ladybugs and two tigers. And then, with Shu Ling's stories drowning out the scampering rats, Wen wasn't afraid anymore.

When the nights got cold and the aunties shut the furnace off to save coal, Wen and Shu Ling huddled in Wen's cot, warming each other. Shu Ling sang the quieter lullabies, one about a jasmine flower, another about a mewing kitten, and another about a bright moon, quiet wind, and a cradle rocking. Often as she listened to Shu Ling's voice, so sweet and delicate, Wen fell asleep. Sometimes, though, when Shu Ling thought Wen was asleep, Wen heard Shu Ling singing herself an old Chinese lullaby:

> Only Mama is the best in all the world.
> With a mama, you have the most valued
>     treasure.
> Jump into Mama's heart and
> You will have endless happiness.

Wen always hoped Shu Ling would fall asleep during that song, which was way too sad for singing.

Even now, as she lay in her new bed in her new room with her new family, Wen listened for Shu Ling's lullabies and the cries of babies waking in the night. This house was too still, and her room was too big. In the darkness, Wen couldn't see the pretty purple of the walls. The big space around her seemed ready to swallow her.

Wen stretched out her arm, still seeking Shu Ling's cot. Her fingers met only air. She listened for Shu Ling's soft, even breathing. The room was silent. She closed her eyes and tried to see Shu Ling's face. She tried to imagine her wide smile and her braid, tied back with a shoelace. But all Wen saw was darkness.

Wen covered her head with her pillow so her new family wouldn't hear her sobs. When she was too tired to cry anymore, she raised her head from under her pillow, got out of bed, and walked across the dark hall to Emily's room. Quietly, she climbed into the cot beside Emily's bed. She pretended Emily's breathing belonged to Shu Ling, sleeping safely beside her after all.

# five

Wen awoke to sunlight streaming across her bed.

Oh, no! She'd forgotten to feed the babies! How had she slept through the big metal gong the aunties rang every morning? *"Quai dian! Quai dian!"* Hurry, Auntie Min and Auntie Lu Chu—the baby aunties—always scolded. Every morning, Wen scurried to the stove, where she stirred the corn porridge, sugar, and water for the babies' bottles. In the next room, the babies wailed. Wen propped up the babies, tilted the bottles against their chests, and slipped the nipples in their tiny mouths so they could drink while she sped to the next aisle. She saw babies raise their limp arms toward her, wanting to be held. *No time*, she would whisper. *Later.*

Now Wen sat upright, listening for the babies. Then she remembered. She was in America.

She heard her father's deep laughter and smelled new, unfamiliar food. Wen rose from her cot in Emily's room, folded her blanket neatly, and arranged it at the foot of the bed. Then she tiptoed down the hall to the kitchen.

*"Ni zao,* Wen," said her mother. "Good morning."

Emily chattered in jumbled English that Wen did not understand. At the stove, her father was frying some brown strips.

"*Ni zao,*" he called over the sizzling of the griddle.

Once Wen sat down, her mother set in front of her a plate heaped with something puffy and yellow, topped with her father's crispy brown strips, still hot.

"Hey, Wen: *bay-con.*"

Wen eyed the crinkled strips, like ribbon, piled on the mountain of yellow fluff. She picked up a slab, took a tiny bite, and then devoured the whole thing.

"Baaaaay-con," Wen repeated. She ate all the yellow fluff and two servings of the crispy bacon, washed down with several glasses of cold milk, so much creamier than the orphanage milk. Then she had two bowls of oatmeal.

"*Ni ha shi e le.* You were hungry." As he read from the card ring, her father patted his rounded belly and smiled at her.

E. Just a tiny word. *Hungry.*

"*E?*" Shu Ling would ask, once she and Wen left the babies and lined up with the other kids down the long hall to the kitchen. Wen nodded, so hungry her stomach rumbled. Usually Cook served the children bowls of dry cornmeal, which they moistened with water from the sink faucet. Sometimes Wen got a hard-boiled egg with some pickled cabbage or a steamed bun. On summer mornings, when there was more food, Wen and the others had noodles or little cat-ear dumplings splashed with vinegar.

Wen and Shu Ling would sit on the cement floor of the common room to eat. Beside them, some of the kids watched American cartoons or Disney movies on the old black-and-white TV that flashed on and off unless you shook it.

Shu Ling always tried to shovel some of her noodles onto Wen's plate because Wen was so tiny, but Wen wanted to give her noodles to Shu Ling, who needed extra strength for walking. They both knew it would be the last food until supper.

Now Wen's mother stood over Wen and showed her a pan of more yellow fluff. With a spoon, she pretended to fill Wen's plate again. Wen shook her head no, but when she thought nobody was looking, she took a banana and a muffin to hide under her shirt, in case she got hungry again.

"Oooooooh!" Emily spotted Wen and aimed her finger at Wen's shirt. Then, in an accusatory tone, she asked her father a question.

Her cheeks burning, Wen tried to bunch her shirt even better over the banana and muffin.

Would they think she was stealing?

Her father glanced at her lumpy shirt, then flipped through some cards on his ring. In faltering Chinese, he read, "*Wo men you hen duo fan.* We have much to eat." Then he pretended to nibble on a muffin. "*Hao ba,* OK, Wen!"

Her hands shaking, Wen put the banana and muffin back.

Of course they thought she was stealing.

After breakfast, Wen went into the bathroom and found a brush, pail, and bleach under the sink. She filled a bucket with water and added bleach and, on her hands and knees, began to scrub the tiles.

"Wen!" said her mother when she saw Wen crouched on the floor. She pulled Wen to her feet. From her bathrobe pocket, her mother fumbled for her card ring. *"Bu biyao. Not necessary."*

She flipped to another card. *"Dao jia le. Home now."*

But this was what Auntie Lan Lan had told her to do. *Remember all the chores. You are a lucky girl. Help them greatly. Otherwise they might send you back.*

Wen's mother led her to her room and opened three bureau drawers, all filled with clothes. From the top drawer, she took out a peach-colored T-shirt and held it against Wen.

For her? Just for her? Wen had never owned a set of clothes.

At the orphanage, Wen had lined up with the other older children to get her clothes on the first day of every week, which they named Day of the Clean Clothes. Auntie Mu Hong, the strictest auntie, decided who got which clothes. As she rummaged through the common wardrobe, she sized up Wen's small body. Wen always closed her eyes and wished for the sparkly Tinker Bell dress or the Hello Kitty shirt. But no, Wen got the boyish clothes, like the Thomas the Tank Engine top or the Batman jersey or the too-big jeans. Auntie Mu Hong bunched up the jeans and pinned them at Wen's waist with a rusty clip. If all the clothes were gone, Wen got one of the faded ruffled nightgowns that hung down to her knees like a sack until seven days passed and another Day of Clean Clothes arrived.

Now, cautiously, Wen took the new T-shirt her mother was offering her. She stroked the soft rosy-peach fabric, the color of a sunset. She had never seen such a beautiful shirt.

Wen gave her mother a small, quick smile.

When Wen's mother smiled back, her eyes sparkled especially blue. All at once, Wen realized that her mother was trying very hard to make her happy.

Wen waited for her mother to go away. Then she pulled a purple tank top over her head and zipped up a pair of jeans. Stretching as tall as she could in front of the mirror on her door, Wen posed in different angles to see how the shirt fell against her body and how her jeans fit, nice and snug along her legs, then flared toward her ankles.

Wen took off the tank top, folded it, and put it back. She changed out of her jeans, too, trying on leggings and a tunic with hearts sewn around the neckline. Wen looked at herself in the mirror. She didn't recognize this girl wearing brand-new clothes that belonged only to her.

Wen slid her hands up and down the flowing fabric and traced the hearts around her neck. Suddenly, in front of the mirror, she pictured Shu Ling beside her, in the torn nightgown.

*Not this one again!* she could hear Shu Ling moan. *What did you get*, mei mei?

Slowly, Wen took off her new outfit. She folded the tunic and leggings, returned them to the drawer, and put on her old denim skirt and sweater again.

When her mother returned, she eyed Wen's wrinkled skirt and stained sweater, then asked her a question. She rattled the bureau and opened the closet, as if she were hunting for the T-shirts and jeans and leggings. Wen opened the top drawer where she'd arranged all the new clothes in neat piles.

"*Buhao?* Bad?" Little lines formed along Wen's mother's forehead.

Wen gazed longingly at the clothes but said nothing. All she could see was Shu Ling in the ragged nightgown.

Her mother tried another card. "*Ni shen ti hao ma?* What's the matter, Wen?"

Wen saw her mother's eyes pleading for an answer.

How could she explain that she liked the clothes so much, her very own clothes? How could she explain that Shu Ling should have them too, and if Shu Ling couldn't have them, neither could she? Wen sat on her bed, making little pleats in her skirt.

"Wen, *hao ba?* OK?" Wen's mother brushed the thick bangs from Wen's eyes.

Wen nodded. She buried her chin in her sweater and pulled away.

Later, in the afternoon, Wen's mother led her to the bathtub and turned on the faucet. In amazement, Wen saw steaming water gush into the tub.

"*Xi zao.* Bath." Beside her, her mother picked up a bar of soap and pretended to rub herself. Wen shrank back. She had never taken a bath. The gleaming white basin in front of her was too long and too shiny, and the water was too deep.

Her mother squirted some blue liquid from a bottle and bubbles burst on the water's surface. Kicking off her shoe, her mother put her foot in the tub. The water stopped below her knee.

"*Hao ba.* It's OK." Her mother pulled her foot out of the water. "*Hao ba* for Wen."

Her mother gave Wen the bar of soap, then flipped through her cards. "*Yi hui jian,*" she read. "See you in a little while." She closed the door behind her.

Wen dipped her bare foot in the hot water. As she pulled out her foot, now dripping, she hesitated. Was that enough to count as a bath?

Cautiously, she took off her clothes, stepped into the foam, and sat. Perfumed bubbles burst around her. Wen stretched her legs along the tub's smooth bottom and let herself slip deeper, until fragrant foam reached her chin.

At the orphanage, Wen and Shu Ling had taken weekly showers along with the other girls in the tiny shower stall. Sometimes girls gawked at Shu Ling's foot and snickered. One day, two new girls had taunted, *Cripple, cripple.* Wen strode through the pelting water and told them to shut up.

The next shower day, while the others slept, Wen led Shu Ling to the kitchen, filled a basin, and brought out a bar of yellow laundry soap. Standing, Shu Ling scrubbed herself until she couldn't reach beyond the top of her bad leg. As Wen stooped to wash the shrunken and twisted part of Shu Ling's leg, they heard footsteps coming down the hall.

"Quick." Wen helped Shu Ling to the floor and they hid behind the sink. From behind the pipes, Wen saw strict Auntie Mu Hong in the doorway. Shaking her head, Auntie Mu Hong clucked disapprovingly, then disappeared.

*Oh, no!* Auntie Mu Hong would tell Director Feng, and he'd mark down in their files that they'd been caught disobeying. Everyone knew that when Director Feng sent names of kids to be adopted in America, he never chose the ones who broke rules. Wen and Shu Ling clung together behind the sink, their eyes joined in fear.

Then Auntie Mu Hong came back, her finger to her lips, and slipped a bottle into Wen's hands. "The lotion will make Shu Ling's leg feel good," Auntie Mu Hong whispered. Then she turned away and closed the kitchen door, so nobody would see.

That evening at dinner, Auntie Mu Hong announced that for medical reasons, Shu Ling would bathe separately from then on.

Wen sat upright in the scented bubbles. Who would wash Shu Ling now? Instantly, the bubbles smelled too strong and the foam made her eyes sting.

Wen stepped out of the water and wrapped herself in a big towel. Back in her bedroom, as she dried herself and put on her old clothes, Wen banged her heel on the trundle bed under her own bed.

*Bed number two*, she thought. *I have an extra bed.*

That was it. She'd ask her own family to adopt Shu Ling! Shu Ling could sleep on the extra bed.

Wen envisioned waking up every morning and rousing Shu Ling. "*Ni zao*," she'd say. "Good morning."

And every single day, Shu Ling would open her eyes, yawn, and say, "*Ni zao, mei mei.*"

Wen started to work out her plan. She would be very good, the best daughter ever. She would do extra chores. She wouldn't eat so much food. She'd be very nice to Emily. Her parents would think about what a wonderful daughter they'd picked. And when she was sure that they wouldn't send her back, she'd ask them to adopt Shu Ling, too.

Wen knew she wouldn't even need much English, when the time came. She'd point everything out, to be sure her mother and father understood. She'd bring them to the extra bed and hold up two fingers. Enough beds. Next she'd pull out a drawer of new clothes and show them. Enough clothes. Then she'd lead her parents to the kitchen and open the refrigerator. Enough food.

Her mother and father would see that they had plenty of room and plenty of clothes and plenty of food—plenty of everything. They would say yes.

Then Wen recalled the story of An Fei.

When An Fei was seven, a family from America had come for her. An Fei's mother and father gave her a teddy bear and hung a silver locket with a photo of their family around her neck. They clasped her tight and said, "We are your forever family." Then An Fei drove away with her new parents.

A week later, a jeep stopped in front of the orphanage and An Fei stepped out. Director Feng called for Auntie Lan Lan to show An Fei back to her old bed. That afternoon, An Fei banged her head against the cement wall until two aunties had to hold her down. Then she lay on her cot and sobbed so loud that every kid in the orphanage heard.

Wen asked Auntie Lan Lan what had happened. Wasn't An Fei adopted anymore?

And Auntie Lan Lan had replied, "No. Disrupted adoption." An Fei's parents had given her back.

"How could those people just give her back?" Wen had asked Auntie Lan Lan.

Auntie Lan Lan replied that An Fei had been a bad girl, not grateful enough. She didn't obey and sometimes she got so mad, she stamped her feet and yelled. And once, when she didn't get what she wanted, she locked herself in her hotel bedroom and wouldn't come out. She never even made it to America.

Then Auntie Lan Lan took Wen's hands and said that there was one thing to know: gratitude. If she ever got picked for adoption, she would be a very lucky girl. She always must be very grateful to the family who chose her. Otherwise, the family might give her back.

"But how will I know?" Wen had asked. "How will I know when I've been good enough?"

"You'll just know in your heart. You'll see a sign," Auntie Lan Lan had said. "Something will happen, maybe something little. But then you'll be sure your family has decided to keep you."

Wen knew she'd have to wait for that sign before she asked her parents to adopt Shu Ling. She would have to be very good and make no demands.

*I'll ask them,* Wen vowed silently. *Not yet. But when I know they've decided to keep me, I'll ask them to adopt Shu Ling, too.*

And of course they'd say yes. She just had to stay alert, so she'd see the keeping sign.

## six

The next day, Wen lay on the living room rug beside Emily, a board of red and black squares between them.

"*Checkers,*" Emily explained, neatly placing black discs on the squares nearest her. After Wen set up the red discs as Emily had demonstrated, Emily began to move her pieces toward Wen's side of the board.

Wen had no idea what she was supposed to do.

Emily said something over and over, then started hopping on her hands and feet, like a frog. "Jump!" she said. "Jump!"

Wen scratched her ear and glanced at Emily, then back to the board of red and black squares.

"No *checkers!*" Emily shook her head, then grinned. She folded up the board and dumped the plastic coins into the box.

Wen shook her head no, too, as she got up from the rug.

"OK . . . book," Emily announced. Snuggling next to Wen on the sofa, Emily put a picture book on Wen's lap. She began flipping the pages, reading to her in halting English words that Wen could not understand.

Wen watched Emily's tiny, upturned face. She liked looking into Emily's dark Chinese eyes, not round like her parents'. She found comfort in Emily's shiny black hair, her bangs cut straight across her forehead. A long look at Emily was a little bit like gazing into a mirror to see her own reflection.

Then she thought of her first sister, Shu Ling.

Wen put the book down and edged away from Emily.

Wen's father stuck his head into the living room, the card ring in his palm. *"Lux ing?"* he read. "Trip?" He put his hands on an imaginary steering wheel as if he were driving.

Wen followed her father, her mother, and Emily into the car and buckled her seat belt the way Emily had showed her. She hated how the seat belt tugged against her. Besides, she didn't even know where they were going.

Suddenly, Wen's father stopped the car in front of a building with a red roof and two yellow arches.

"McDonald's!" Wen shouted. She recognized McDonald's from the trip she'd taken with Ying Ying's new parents back in China.

"Hey, Wennie knows McDonald's!" Emily exclaimed.

Wen followed her family to a long line inside. When she got to the counter, Wen pointed to the picture of a hamburger and fries. At their booth, Wen's father got out his silver camera and set it beside his tray. Wen bit into her hamburger and then, her mouth opened wide, finished the whole thing. She devoured her french fries, which she'd smothered in ketchup, camera and took a photo.

"You like?" Her mother cut her own hai and offered it to Wen.

"I like McDonald's." Hearing her own word choked on the burger. A whole sentence! Maybe English was finally coming back.

"Wennie talked!" Emily waved a chicken nugget in the air.

"What a surprise! You knew some English all along!" Wen's mother said.

Her father gave her a thumbs-up. Wen knew what this meant, because kids at the orphanage gave one another thumbs-up too, to say *great job*. Wen grinned proudly at her dad.

"I hungry," Wen said, almost as if she were practicing with Auntie Lan Lan. "Now I not hungry much."

"Wennie talked again." Emily dumped more french fries on Wen's tray.

"You must know a lot of English, Wen!" said her mother.

"Little bit." Wen reached for a fry.

Wen's father took a final swig of his drink, picked up his cup, and went over to a big machine that spurted out soda. He filled his cup to the brim.

Wen opened her eyes wide. "More? My father, she *steal*?"

Emily burst out laughing. "Dad is a *he*. And Wennie, refills are free."

ree?" Wen hesitated. "What is this, free?"

"More is OK." Taking Wen's hand, Emily walked Wen to the drink machine, where she taught her how to push her cup against a metal clasp until soda streamed out. Wen went back to fill her cup again and again. Finishing her third drink, she heard a chime coming from her mother's purse. Wen looked around for bells.

"My phone!" Her mother took out a small silver object, flipped it open, and began to talk.

"Cell phone, Wen." Emily put a pretend phone to her ear. "People carry. Everybody has them, even big kids."

"Cell phone," Wen repeated. Director Feng had a cell phone, but he was always complaining about it. "Bad reception!" he'd shout, pounding the keys with his thick fingers. Wen had never seen a cell phone up close.

"Sorry. I hate to take calls on the weekend, but this was for work." Her mother shut her phone and tossed it back into her purse.

As they left the restaurant, a woman kept the door open for them.

"Excuse me," Wen's father said. "Can I ask you to take our picture?" He lent her his camera.

Wen's mother arranged everybody standing against the McDonald's wall.

"Say cheese," said her father.

What was her father talking about? Cheese was for eating, not taking photographs.

The lady snapped two poses and gave the camera back to Wen's father, who grinned at the shots on the digital screen.

"What a family!" He pushed back his Red Sox cap and beamed.

Wen peeked over the camera to see. The photos were a lot like the one her family had sent when she lived at the orphanage, except now she was in there too, with a little curve of a smile on her face. Behind her, her mother rested her chin on the top of Wen's head, her arm around one shoulder, her father's arm around the other, while Emily squeezed her hand.

Wen hadn't really believed it before. But there she was, surrounded by her mother, her father, and Emily. A normal girl with her own family.

Only it wasn't a complete family, she reminded herself. Not yet. Not without Shu Ling.

The next day, Wen's mother flipped through the ring of cards and tapped her wristwatch. *"Peng you* coming. Soon," she told Wen.

*Friend?* Wen raised her eyebrows. She didn't have any friends here.

"It's Nancy Lin," Emily explained. "The adoption lady."

Wen had never heard of adoption ladies in America.

What would this lady do? Decide if she was good enough?

Suppose the adoption lady came into her bedroom? Frantic, Wen ran to her room to straighten her sheets, smoothing out all the little hills and valleys her comforter had made. Then she lined up her sneakers and rearranged her books.

"Wen!" she heard her mother call. "Come meet Nancy Lin."

Holding her breath, Wen walked down the hall.

"*Jian dao ni hen gao xing!* I'm glad to meet you, Wen!" a Chinese woman with short-cropped hair said. "You are even more beautiful than your photo!" She clasped Wen's hand in hers.

Wen blinked. It was odd to see a Chinese woman not wearing a starched white auntie coat.

"*Jian dao ni hen gao xing!*" Wen said, hearing her own Chinese flow smoothly. Wen shook the lady's hand and bowed slightly, her right fist against her waist, the way all the children were taught to bow to Director Feng.

*Don't send me back.* Wen tried to stay perfectly still. *I haven't had enough time to be as good as I can be. I should have called Emily* mei mei, *even once. I shouldn't have taken the banana and muffin. I should have worn those clothes my mother bought me, instead of changing back into my old skirt and sweater. And I never should have eaten that half hamburger from my mother's plate.*

"Nancy helped us adopt Emily, then you." Her mother gazed toward Emily and then toward Wen. Her eyes sparkled so brightly, they lit up her whole face, radiant as the sun.

"My two daughters!" her mother said, her voice thick, like she might cry or something.

"Such wonderful daughters, too," Nancy added.

Wen's mother asked Nancy to stay and have some tea.

"No, no, Chris, nothing for me! I can't stay long. I just wanted to meet Wen. I'll be back soon," she said, buttoning her coat.

"We'll have you over for dinner. Richard wants to see you too!" her mother said.

"I'll e-mail you with dates." Nancy and Wen's mother hugged.

As Wen heard Nancy drive away, she went into her room and sunk into her neatly made bed. That was a close call. Nancy hadn't mentioned sending her back this time. But she could have.

Now this adoption lady Nancy was going to be calling, and coming by to spy on her, and even eating dinner with her. Wen knew she had to be on guard, a better daughter than ever.

# seven

"Wennie, I got to miss a whole week of school because we were getting you!" Emily skipped beside Wen and her mother down the street to the bus stop on Monday morning.

When a yellow bus arrived, Emily scrambled up the stairs, behind all the big kids. As the bus pulled away, she waved through the window at Wen and her mother.

"I go?" Wen asked as they headed for home. "This is possible, soon?"

"It's the third week in September." Her mother fumbled for the card ring. *"Duo zai jia dai zhe?* Stay home longer? Learn more English." Her mother put her palms together and opened them, like a book.

"Thank you," Wen said. "But know much now," she added.

"Learn more words with me first?" her mother asked. "I don't have to be back to work until next month."

Wen turned away to hide her frown. She didn't want to stay home with her mother. She wanted to go to school.

Auntie Lan Lan had told her about the schools in

America. The floors were as shiny as glass and towers of books were stacked from the floor to the ceiling. All the kids got their own desks and their own computers. If you studied hard at school in America, when you grew up, you could get a good job and become very rich.

"I go to school yesterday," said Wen.

"You mean tomorrow?" her mother asked, pushing her long fingers through her frizzy hair.

Wen saw her mother's chest rise as she sighed in disappointment. But more clearly, in her mind, she pictured the classroom waiting for her at the end of the bus line.

"School, thank you," said Wen.

"I'll have to call the teachers. They aren't expecting you for a few more weeks, Wen." Wen's mother put an imaginary phone to her ear.

"OK," said Wen. "Please tell them, coming more soon. Could tell them, tomorrow."

When they got back home, Wen heard her mother talking on the phone, then hanging up.

"I got it cleared, Wen. The school says you can start tomorrow. You're sure you're ready?"

"Oh, yes!" Wen exclaimed. "Much ready."

That night, Wen's mother came in to say good night and kiss her pillow. *She got you into school early; you should be grateful,* Wen thought as she gazed into her mother's blue eyes. Still, Wen couldn't let her face get so close to her mother's, and she rolled over.

"Thank you," she wanted to whisper. But instead she buried her head under the pillow until her mother left the room.

Tomorrow she was going to school in America!

$$\smile\!\!\smile$$

The next morning, Wen couldn't decide which of her new clothes to wear. Finally she picked out the peach colored T-shirt, the deep purple tank top, and the bright yellow tunic with hearts all along the neckline. Wen wore all of them, one on top of the other.

"That's a lot of shirts," her mother commented as Wen sat down for breakfast.

Wen pretended she didn't hear her. Instead, she bent her chin to see the pretty hearts near her neck. These three shirts belonged all to her, and she would wear every one.

Her mother touched one of Wen's sleeves. "One, two, three," she counted slowly. "Too many shirts. The other girls won't be wearing so many."

"Like all." Wen chewed her bacon, wishing her mother would stop peering, with those deep worry wrinkles around her eyes, at her three beautiful shirts. She left the table and got her backpack.

"I'll drive you to school today and pick you up, since it's your first day." Her mother jingled the car keys.

"Bus, please?" said Wen. Just like Emily and the other kids.

"Tomorrow." Her mother pressed her thin lips together, which Wen knew meant she was being firm.

They got into the car and soon swung into the school parking lot. Wen observed the long, low building made of beige brick. A red, white, and blue flag fluttered from a tall pole at the entrance.

An American school right in front of her! And she was going inside!

"This way, Wen. We're early." Wen's mother led her through a long hall to a room that said SIXTH GRADE. A willowy woman with wavy gray hair met them at the door.

"Ms. Beckwith, this is my daughter, Wen McGuire," said Wen's mother.

"Good morning, Wen," Ms. Beckwith said. "Welcome!" While she shook hands with Ms. Beckwith, Wen peeked at the classroom. It was more magical than she had ever dreamed.

Desks with smooth tops were grouped in squares of four. In the back, a whole bookshelf sagged with books, right beside two stuffed chairs. Just like Auntie Lan Lan had said, the floors were so shiny Wen could catch the reflection of her new sneakers.

"Wen, I'm going now." Her mother tilted her head toward the door. "Back at three." Showing Wen her watch, she raised three fingers. "*Zai jian.*"

*Zai jian?* Her mother leaving? Wen clamped her knees tight to keep her legs steady.

Of course she had known her mother was leaving. She didn't even stay with Emily. *You knew this was coming,* Wen scolded herself.

"Here's where you'll sit, Wen." Ms. Beckwith took her to a seat by the window. Wen stroked the glassy top of the brand-new desk, with a space for books underneath. Her own desk, all hers!

In the tiny, dim orphanage classroom, Wen and the other students had squeezed onto a splintery bench by a long table. In front, Teacher Jun scratched Chinese characters on a blackboard. Wen copied the characters into her small notebook, her back sore from sitting so straight for so long.

Now as she settled into her shiny American desk, Wen heard a bell and kids shouting high-pitched English in the hallway. Coming toward her, a girl with a thick blonde ponytail and tight jeans chattered with another girl in a baggy sweatshirt, her reddish bangs nearly covering her eyes. The girls sat down at the two desks opposite Wen's. Then a girl with tangled brown hair came flying through the door, a piece of buttered toast in her hand.

"The alarm didn't go off this morning!" She plopped down at the desk beside Wen's, her notebooks and pencil scattering on the floor.

"Hey, Hannah!" The blonde girl scooped up the pencil and returned it to her.

"Thanks. How's it going, Michelle?" The late girl ate the last crust of her toast and then grinned, revealing teeth that sparkled like little stars.

Wen forced herself not to stare. But then, out of the corner of her eye, she peeked again. The girl had silver bands on each tooth. Wen had never seen such sparkly teeth.

"You must be the new girl. We heard you were coming today." She directed a wide, glittering smile at Wen. "I'm Hannah. And she's Michelle."

"Hi." Wen heard her own voice, very faint and small.

The blonde girl didn't bother to look up.

Ignored by Michelle, Wen felt herself shrink smaller than she really was, almost invisible.

"I'm Sophie," said the redheaded girl.

Ms. Beckwith clapped her hands and the kids got quiet. "Good morning," she said, smiling broadly at Wen as she continued to speak. Wen caught the words "Wen McGuire," and "new student from China."

Wen felt the other kids' eyes inspecting her and slid lower in her chair. Did she look OK? Were her hair clumps flat? Would the other kids like her?

"Another new kid?" a boy near her groaned.

Wen wanted to sink right through that shiny floor and disappear.

"What's up with all those shirts?" Michelle asked, her eyebrows arched.

Wen crossed her arms over her pretty shirts, as if to protect herself. What would this mean girl say to her next?

Unexpectedly, a large, cheerful voice came booming from the sky. "Good morning," said a pleasant lady overhead. Startled, Wen sat up, but she didn't see anyone. It took her a moment to realize that the words were coming out of a box near the ceiling.

Then Ms. Beckwith and the whole class stood up, faced an American flag that was hanging in the corner, and put their hands on their hearts. Wen scrambled to her feet, her own hand over her own heart. In unison, the kids recited some words. Maybe it was a poem, like the Tang poems Teacher Jun made them repeat until they said the lines just right. The only words Wen recognized were "The United States of America." Just as quickly as they'd gotten up, all the kids sat down, and that was that. Nobody talked about the poem. Maybe it was a special festival day or something.

Ms. Beckwith picked up a big textbook and the kids got out matching books from the space under their desks. Ms. Beckwith passed Wen her own book. Wen flipped the pages, which were mainly pictures of maps. Then Ms. Beckwith asked a question, and the kids took turns giving answers that Wen didn't understand.

Wen strained hard to pick up any English she knew. The

words seemed to buzz, like flies swarming over the babies' heads on the hottest days. Wen's skin was wet under her three shirts.

Finally Ms. Beckwith said "lunchtime." The kids pushed their chairs from their desks and scrambled to their lockers to get their lunches and head down the hall. Wen followed.

When she reached a big room filled with rows of long tables, Wen stopped in the doorway. Hannah and Michelle joined Sophie and two other girls at a nearby table and spread out their lunches. They unwrapped pieces of white bread stuck together with jelly, and sipped from straws sticking out of little boxes. Hannah beckoned toward Wen but before she could move, other girls had taken the empty seats. Hannah seemed to be telling a story, waving her hands through the air. The girls around her listened intently, their eyes tracking her as she talked.

Wen ate her noodles at a table in the back, alone.

When lunch was over, Wen went back to class and waited for Ms. Beckwith to start speaking more English. From her fringed sack, Michelle took out a cell phone just like Wen's mother's, only hot pink. Hannah fumbled for her own phone in the back of her desk.

"Hannah, I picked a cool new ringtone for you." Michelle flipped open her phone. "Turn on your phone, and I'll show you." She pushed a button and Hannah's phone burst into catchy, loud music.

"Girls, no cell phones in class." Ms. Beckwith towered

over Michelle's desk. "Turn those off right now before I take them for the rest of the day."

Then Ms. Beckwith gave some sort of order to the class. All the kids got up from their chairs. Not knowing where she was going, Wen filed behind Hannah and Michelle until the line stopped.

Wen read a sign over the door: ART ROOM.

Once inside, Wen reeled. The room was three times larger than the common room back at the orphanage. Sunlight streamed through the windows. Overhead, wire shapes of birds and butterflies hung from thin strings. One whole wall was lined with sculptures made of rich brown clay. Another wall held jars of paint in colors Wen had never seen before—greens like apples and early spring leaves, blood-reds, sparkly golds, and oranges as deep as setting suns.

*If only Shu Ling could be in this room!* Wen thought. *Just think of the pictures she could draw here.*

A lady in a paint-spattered smock directed kids to big pieces of paper hanging on stands. Wen dipped her brush into the blue paint beside her. Slowly, she made a blue circle on the blank paper. Then she painted another loop, this one covering the first. With each circle, Wen imagined Shu Ling, holding the paintbrush just right, her eyes dazzling as she covered the smooth paper with floating lotus blossoms or fireworks on the Lunar New Year. The more she missed Shu Ling, the bigger she painted her circles. Soon her paper was a mass of dripping blue swirls.

"Blue circles. How original!" Michelle said with a smirk as she passed Wen on the way to the sink.

Wen blushed. Now her swirls seemed babyish and silly, something a toddler would do. Wen raised her brush to the paper, but she couldn't paint anymore. As she tried to hide her picture behind her, her eyes darted around the room. Suppose Michelle came back again?

When the kids returned to the classroom, Wen heard more scrambled English. When a shrill bell rang at three o'clock, kids all leapt from their desks and tore out the door.

At last! School was over! At the main entrance, Wen watched for her mother's gray car. Minutes passed, each one seeming longer than the one before.

An unexpected chill came over Wen.

As she sat against the brick wall, Wen's back throbbed the way it had hurt when her first mother had propped her against the bag of noodles at the orphanage gate.

Then she knew: Her mother wasn't coming.

Wen got up from the steps. As if in a trance, she walked into the street to see better. Suddenly, Wen heard a screech. In front of her, a big green van jerked to a halt.

"Watch out!" The man behind the wheel honked the horn. "Are you crazy? I nearly hit you."

For an instant, Wen froze. Her heart pounding, she

sprinted back to the sidewalk and huddled against the school wall.

Just then, her mother's car pulled up at the curb.

"Wen, I'm over here," her mother called from the driver's seat. "I got stuck in traffic. Sorry I'm a little late."

Wen got up from the wall, her back still sore, her legs shaking. In measured steps, Wen walked to the car. She climbed into the front seat quickly so her mother wouldn't see her trembling.

"How was your first day?" her mother asked.

Wen clasped her hands tight in her lap.

"What is it, Wen? You're so quiet. Did something bad happen today?"

Wen said nothing. What was bad was her mother leaving her like that in front of the school, all alone.

At the stop sign, Wen's mother grasped Wen's fingers. "Honey, you're freezing!" Wen's mother pretended to shiver. "Cold?"

"Not cold." Wen turned to the window.

"Honey, tell me," her mother said.

"Hey, you very late." Wen kept the back of her head to her mother. "Almost you not come."

"I know. I was about five minutes late." Her mother raised five fingers. "I'm really sorry, sweetie."

"Not five. Very late. You I not see." Wen talked to the glass.

"I'm so sorry, Wen. You must have been worried." Her mother's voice wavered.

"I not worry."

Wen's mother stopped the car in front of their house. Gingerly, she reached for Wen's chin and held her face in her hands.

"Look at me," her mother said, still holding Wen's chin, so that Wen had to lock her eyes right onto her mother's.

"I will always come for you, do you understand, Wen? I always come."

Wen turned her chin away. It wasn't true. Her mother didn't always come. She almost didn't come that afternoon.

"I not worry," Wen said. Then she edged away from her mother and stared at the window, not speaking.

# eight

That night at dinner, Wen's mother handed her a silver cell phone. "Dad and I got you this so you can call if you need us."

Wen inspected the sleek phone in her palm. Her parents had bought this so she wouldn't worry, like this afternoon. Were they annoyed she caused them to buy her a fancy new phone?

"How come she gets a cell phone and I don't?" Emily asked. "It's not fair!"

"Because she's new to everything here and may want to call us," said their father.

"Suppose I need you?" Emily demanded. "She gets one just because she's new?"

"Calm down, Emily," their mother warned, glancing uneasily at Wen. "You're only in second grade, sweetie. You're too young for a cell phone."

"All you ever do is pay attention to Wen," Emily whined. "Don't I count anymore?"

Wen saw Emily's eyes brim with tears, as if she were about to cry. She couldn't make Emily cry.

"You can try mine," Wen offered.

"Come on, Emily, of course you count." Wen's mother rubbed Emily's back. "We have lots of love to go around for everybody. We have to help Wen until she gets used to things, that's all."

Wen put her face in her hands. She had made Emily mad. She had gotten her parents upset. She had caused too much trouble.

Then Wen felt her father's hands pry her fingers, gingerly, one by one, off her face. "It's OK, Wen," said her father. "Emily's just a little upset, that's all. We're all really glad you're here. Aren't we, Emily?"

Emily picked at her macaroni and cheese and said nothing.

After dinner, Wen went into her bedroom. In the kitchen, she could hear her parents both speaking in lowered tones with Emily. Were they talking about her?

They were going to send her back. Maybe she'd upset Emily so badly her parents had decided they couldn't have two daughters after all. And they loved Emily the best. Of course they did. Emily was first. So Wen had to go.

At breakfast the next morning Wen waited for her mother or father to announce that they'd decided it was time for her to pack her things. Instead, her mother cheerfully poured her orange juice and Emily was busy stirring raisins into her oatmeal. Wen nibbled on her toast and passed Emily the milk even before she asked.

That morning, she took the school bus for the first time. She sat with Emily, who seemed to have forgotten all about the night before. Emily bounced up and down on the seat.

"See, Wennie, aren't buses fun?"

Later, at her new desk, Wen took her phone out of her pocket and set it right in the middle of her desk, hoping that the nice girl, Hannah, would notice and get her number. Maybe the other girls would ask too. Hannah and Sophie were already at their seats. Just as Hannah turned toward Wen, Michelle rushed into the room.

"Hey, check out what I got!" Michelle arched her body to show off a light blue jacket with no sleeves, its edges lined in white fuzz.

*Why would a jacket have no sleeves?* Wen wondered.

"Don't worry, the vest is fake fur. It's not from a killed animal or anything." She tossed her blonde hair off her shoulders.

Wen kept her eyes on her silver phone, gleaming in the middle of her desk. Nobody noticed or asked for her number. What good was a cell phone if you had nobody to call? She pushed it to the back of her desk, hidden under her extra sweatshirt and English book.

At recess, by the fence, Wen saw Hannah, Michelle, and Sophie gathered under a big tree. Michelle was weaving Hannah's hair into two thick braids.

Wen could almost feel Shu Ling's hair, heavy in her fingers. Every spring, Wen and Shu Ling had climbed past the gully to the peony fields. They gathered the big blossoms, their soft pink petals radiant in the sunlight. Then they took turns lacing the flowers into each other's hair. When they returned to the orphanage, they kept some peonies in their pockets, to dry, until the next spring came.

Now as she watched Hannah, Michelle, and Sophie braid one another's hair, Wen could almost smell the sweetness of the peonies lingering as she sat, all alone, on the grass.

That afternoon, Wen took the bus home, with Emily beside her, chattering about something so fast that Wen could barely make out her words. All around her, Wen heard kids shouting. As the bus swerved around corners, she clung to Emily so she wouldn't fall off her seat.

When she got home that afternoon, Wen saw her mother in the kitchen, waiting for her. "How was school today?" she asked.

"OK." Wen avoided her mother's eager gaze.

Wen went into the backyard and scuffed through the fallen leaves. The harder she kicked, the more brown leaves scattered into the air, making a dry, rustling sound before they fell back to the ground.

Then, at the far end of the backyard, Wen noticed a tiny hill, like the dusty space in back of the orphanage. Wen climbed the hill, pretending she was walking toward Shu Ling. When she made it to the top, she stopped, and then began to spin.

As she spun, she could practically see Shu Ling perched

on the old tires. The spinning game, they had called it. Wen would stand straight as a reed, spread both arms, and begin to twirl. Every time she spun by Shu Ling, she fixed her eyes on her. Catching Shu Ling's face every rotation helped her keep her balance. When she got too dizzy, she collapsed on the dirt, her head whirring, her eyes closed. Finally, she would open her eyes to see Shu Ling, hovering over her.

"Faster than ever, *mei mei*," Shu Ling always said. "Fastest yet."

Now as she whirled, she tried to imagine Shu Ling, anchoring her. But instead she just caught glimpses of folded-up lawn chairs and the neighbor's tall wooden fence. She pivoted twice before, like a twirling plate slowing down, she wobbled and fell.

Wen lay still on the cold ground. Then, with both hands, she heaped piles of leaves over her body, burying herself. Leaf tips pricked her skin. The wet leaves smelled moldy and her back felt damp against the dirt.

"Wen!" her father shouted.

"Richard," Wen heard her mother say, her voice frantic, "where can she be?"

She heard the back door open, followed by the sound of footsteps. Through the leaves, Wen saw a pair of brown boots. Then she felt her father's hand reaching down to find hers.

"Here you are, Wen! Come on, let me help you up." Wen

took his wrist and let him pull her up from the ground. Then, together, they went inside.

Wen's mother made room beside her on the sofa. "Sit."

"Rug dirty now," Wen said.

Her mother smoothed Wen's hair. "What's wrong, Wen? Sad?" With her fingers, she made pretend tears along her own cheeks.

"Not sad. OK." Wen moved away from her mother.

"You can tell us, Wen," her father said. "What is it?"

Of course, Wen couldn't say. Instead, she took her cell phone out of her pocket. "Hey, how far this phone make call?" she asked.

"How far? Anywhere in the United States, I guess," her mother said.

Wen wanted to ask *Can this cell phone reach China?* But of course it couldn't. And besides, even if the phone did get China, maybe a call would cost too much money.

If she just asked, would her parents think she was being greedy?

"Even more far?" She had to know.

Wen's mother pushed her glasses on top of her head, as if something had just occurred to her. "Would you like to call the orphanage, Wen? You must be missing your friends there."

Wen gripped her cell phone. Call Shu Ling? Hear her voice again? "This I could do?" asked Wen.

"I'll ask Nancy to see if you can get permission," said her

mother. She got up to call from the landline hanging on the wall in the kitchen.

Wen's father held up his crossed fingers.

"Why you do this?" asked Wen.

"Means 'make a wish,'" said her father.

"Wish for call." Wen crossed her fingers too.

Wen heard her mother speaking with someone in a low voice.

"Wen," she said, "Nancy wants to talk with you."

Why would this adoption lady want to talk to her? Was there something wrong with calling the orphanage after you'd left? Did you get sent back for something like that?

When Wen reached the kitchen, her mother handed her the phone.

"Hello?" Wen said.

"Hello, Wen, this is Nancy. I wanted to tell you how sorry I am that you are missing your friends at the orphanage. It's very hard at first, Wen. I see this with the older kids. And I want you to know, if I can help in any way, you must call me."

The warmth in Nancy's voice made Wen want to cry.

"So I can call today?" Wen asked. "It is OK?"

"*Shi de.* Yes!" Nancy said. "Director Feng allows calls at first. I gave your mother the phone number."

"Thank you," Wen said, almost singing. "Oh, *xie xie!* Thank you!" Then she hung up.

She wanted to throw her arms around her mother and

thank her for calling Nancy Lin. But when she thought of touching her mother, something inside her stirred and said *danger*.

"I call now?" Wen asked.

"Well, we're about twelve hours behind China time right now. So if you call tonight at seven, it'll be seven tomorrow morning at the orphanage," said her mother.

"What you say?" Wen asked. "Seven and seven?"

Her mother tapped her wristwatch. "At seven here, we eat dinner. But China is on the other side of the world." She waved her arms, as if gesturing toward somewhere far away. "When it's seven at night here, it's seven in the morning in China."

"Friend up then!"

"Which friend, sweetie? What's her name?" her mother asked.

Wen hesitated. Should she tell them about Shu Ling so soon? She might start to cry. She didn't want her parents to see her upset and think she wasn't grateful for being in their family.

"Friend's name is Shu Ling," Wen started. "She is my best friend."

"Have you been friends for a long time?" her father asked.

"Very long time." Her voice cracked. That was all she could say for now.

So instead, Wen began to walk up and down the hall.

"Pacing like that won't help." Her mother handed her a potato. "Here, help me finish dinner while Dad goes to pick up Emily from her playdate."

Silently, Wen scraped the potato, watching its skin fall off in long, thin curls.

"Your friend, Shu Ling." Her mother glanced up from seasoning the tomato sauce. "You must miss her very much."

Wen didn't answer. How could she tell her mother that without Shu Ling, part of her still stayed back at the orphanage? How could she describe how she strained at night, listening for Shu Ling's breathing, and heard only her own heart beating? And how could she say that sometimes she stood still, waiting for Shu Ling to rest her arm on her shoulder, and felt nothing but the weight of her own sadness? Wen couldn't peel herself open that way in front of her mother.

"Potatoes done." She slid the cutting board toward her mother.

At dinner, Wen couldn't eat.

Finally it was time. "Seven!" Wen called. "Hey, it's seven!"

Wen's mother showed Wen a piece of paper with many numbers. Her mother told her to use the landline, because it worked better, and to dial very slowly.

Wen cradled the receiver to her chest. She could almost hear Shu Ling's voice saying, "Mei mei, *you called!*"

And then she'd say, *How are you, Shu Ling?* and *I miss you so much* and *Who do you play with now?* and *Have you had any cat-ear dumplings yet?* and *Did any new babies come in?*

As she pushed the buttons on the phone, one by one, Wen's fingers shook.

The phone rang for a long time. *Wasn't anybody there?*

Finally she heard a click, followed by a loud "*Ni hao.* Hello."

"Auntie Lan Lan!" Wen shrieked. "It's me, Wen!"

"Ah, Wen!" Auntie Lan Lan answered. "How is America?"

Auntie Lan Lan sounded very far away. Wen raised her voice. It felt good to be speaking her own language. "America is great, Auntie Lan Lan, and my English came back," said Wen. "And the school has shiny floors, just like you said."

"I knew it!" said Auntie Lan Lan. "You are getting smarter every day. Soon you'll be rich, too."

"Can I talk to Shu Ling?" asked Wen.

After a moment, Wen heard the low voice she knew so well. "*Mei mei?*"

"Shu Ling!" Wen shouted.

Shu Ling whispered something.

"Talk louder, Shu Ling!" Wen said.

"How are you, *mei mei?*" she asked softly.

"I miss you," said Wen.

Shu Ling got very quiet. Then Wen heard her begin to sob.

"Shu Ling, please don't." Wen gripped the receiver.

"Oh, *mei mei,*" Shu Ling choked.

"What is it, Shu Ling? Are you still there?" Wen asked.

Shu Ling didn't speak.

"Shu Ling, say something!" Wen begged.

Finally Wen heard Shu Ling let out a long cry, almost a moan. The phone dropped with a thud.

"Wen, it's Auntie Lan Lan again. Shu Ling can't talk anymore."

"Why not?" Wen fought back her tears.

"She's too upset, I think. She's going back in her cot to lie down. She misses you too much right now. Maybe writing is better, Wen."

"But I miss her too, Auntie Lan Lan. Can't you tell her to come back? I want to talk to her!"

"She cannot, Wen. Try to understand. It is too much for her. I have to hang up now, the babies are waiting. Be sure to be a good girl, Wen. Good-bye."

Wen heard the line go dead. She kept the phone in her hand, hoping it would ring again and Auntie Lan Lan would say, *She's here again. Shu Ling can talk after all.*

But the phone stayed silent. Wen imagined Shu Ling in her cot back at the orphanage.

Then, feeling as sad and as still as Shu Ling, she walked down the hall and climbed into her own bed, tucking her body into a curve, just the way Shu Ling did.

# nine

*"Dear Shu Ling . . ."* On notebook paper, Wen slanted her calligraphy pen to form curving Chinese characters. She reminded herself to start her letter simply, the way she had when she'd taught Shu Ling how to read and write.

One day in the fall after Wen had come to the orphanage, Auntie Lan Lan rang the gong and lined up the six-year-old boys and girls in the courtyard. If Director Feng tapped their heads, they would go to school in the classroom on the second floor. But the kids whose heads he didn't tap would stay back and help with the babies.

Director Feng walked up and down the row of six-year-olds. *Pick me,* Wen begged silently. *Pick me!* She felt a pat on her head. She'd been picked!

"I wish you could go to school too," Wen told Shu Ling that afternoon.

"There would be no point. Director Feng says I'm 'defective,' *mei mei,*" Shu Ling said.

"Stupid word." Wen seethed. "Stupid."

Wen had stormed over to Director Feng's office, raised her arm, and knocked. Director Feng came to the door and glared. "Why can't Shu Ling go to school?" Wen asked, wishing her voice sounded bigger and braver.

Director Feng told Wen that it was not her place to question him. Children with disabilities like Shu Ling had no future, and he couldn't waste money educating them. He reminded her that children who questioned their elders did not get chosen for adoption. He slammed his door shut.

Wen started school in the dark classroom upstairs while Shu Ling fed the babies, pulled weeds, and scrubbed the bathroom floors. Each afternoon, when school was over, Wen taught Shu Ling what she'd learned that day. On their hill, Wen used a stick to scratch Chinese characters in the dust. In a few months, Wen and Shu Ling were reading simple words together. They began writing secret notes for each other, hidden in the rim of a tire. Sometimes Shu Ling gave her drawings. Once, Shu Ling had left a picture of yellow chrysanthemums; another time, a sketch of a baby sleeping, the sun filtering across her gaunt cheeks. Wen folded the pictures under her mattress and considered them treasures.

Now Wen had so much to tell Shu Ling.

Dear Shu Ling,

I am sorry that my phone call made you so sad. Maybe we should write letters instead.

How are you? I miss you so much. How is everybody there? How are the babies doing? Who do you play with on the hill now? At recess, the girls all sit in groups together. They don't pay much attention to me.

We won't have to write letters for too long, because I have a plan for getting you a family. My own family! Sometimes I get a little scared of them. They can still seem like strange Americans. Plus sometimes they speak English so fast I have no idea what they're saying.

But I have a plan. I'm going to be really good, not greedy, until I see a sign that my family has decided to keep me. Once I know that, I'll ask them to adopt you! I even have another bed, right under mine. Give me a month or so. Then it will be your lucky day too!

Please write back.

Love from your mei mei,

Wen

P.S. The other day we went to McDonald's. Do you remember when the Americans took us there and we got a prize with our Happy Meals? I remember how we both got sparkly rings with great big plastic diamonds and how we put those huge rings on our fingers and flicked our hands in the sunlight and made little rainbows all over the McDonald's!

"Hey, have small question for you," Wen called down the hall to her mother. "How send letter to China?"

"You're writing to Shu Ling?" As her mother came into her bedroom, Wen was just sealing the envelope. She glanced at the portrait Wen had tacked over her desk. "This must be you and Shu Ling, right?" she asked.

Pushing her chair back a little, Wen let her mother see.

"She seems like a nice girl. Such kind eyes! And you two look like very good friends."

Wen felt tears coming. Quickly, she pulled her chair closer to the desk, to block her mother's view. She'd seen Shu Ling enough.

Maybe now was the time to ask. "Such a nice girl," her mother had said. It would be so easy to say, "So nice, would you adopt her?"

But there had been no hint that her parents would keep her forever. When would she see the sign Auntie Lan Lan had told her about?

"Maybe you could send her a package, too. Package . . ." Her mother etched a box on a piece of paper. Wen noticed that her mother had stopped using the ring of cards and was acting things out or drawing the words instead. Sometimes Wen secretly smiled at her mother's clumsy sketches. Still, the pictures were more fun than cards.

"Maybe new clothes." Wen's mother sketched a T-shirt.

"Oh, Shu Ling like new clothes!" Wen exclaimed.

That afternoon, Wen's mother drove Wen and Emily to the mall to shop for Shu Ling.

"What mall is?" Wen stood between her mother and Emily as a door to the building opened all by itself.

"You'll see." Emily grabbed Wen's hand.

They entered a magic place covered with a curved glass ceiling. Wen gazed all around her and gasped. Were these leafy trees growing beside the splashing fountain real? How could the water shoot upward so high, making little droplets that sparkled in the sun?

And the stores! Wen had never seen so many stores, all with huge windows where pretend people with no faces posed in beautiful new clothes.

"Let's go to the toy store first," Emily begged.

In the first aisle, Wen saw rows of Barbie dolls, some dressed as princesses, brides, or doctors. At the orphanage, Auntie Mu Hong distributed the Barbie, the hula hoop, and the plastic dump truck so that everybody had a turn with a real toy. The others played tag among the shrubs or tossed pebbles in the courtyard.

Whenever Wen and Shu Ling got the Barbie, they headed for their dusty space to play the choosing game. Walking the Barbie through the air, Shu Ling would say, "Which kid should I pick?" She'd stop right by Wen. "I choose you!" the Barbie would say, her little plastic hand tapping Wen on the head. Next, Wen got to grasp the Barbie and finally decide on Shu Ling.

Now Wen felt a tug on her arm. *"Wen-nie,* what's the matter?" she heard Emily's little voice ask. "Do you want Mommy to buy you a Barbie?"

Wen envisioned Shu Ling, eyes wide in delight, as she lifted her own Princess Barbie from the plastic wrapping. She'd take the Barbie by her skinny waist and stroke her glittery princess dress, billowing to her delicately curved feet. Then she'd comb Barbie's long blonde hair with her fingers and caress Barbie's jeweled crown.

But whom would she play with? How could Shu Ling play the choosing game if there was nobody to pick her?

"Wennie, what is it? You want Mommy to buy your *friend* a Barbie?" Emily tugged at Wen's shirt.

"Shu Ling not need Barbie," said Wen.

Wen followed her mother and Emily up the moving stairs to a big store where girls' shirts were arranged in neat stacks.

"Pick one?" Wen asked.

"Three," said her mother.

Careful not to mess up the rows, Wen pored through the shirts. Finally she picked a bright red tunic. *Red for good luck,* she thought. Then she chose a fuzzy, deep-blue sweater and a long-sleeved jersey with sparkly swirls all over the front.

On the way home, in the passenger seat by her mother, Wen held the bag of shirts, wrapped in tissue, in her lap. If Auntie Mu Hong, who was in charge of all the clothing, got to the shirts first, she'd cram them into the common wardrobe, to be shared with all the other girls. But if Auntie Lan Lan opened the shirts, she'd let Shu Ling have them, maybe hiding them under her blanket.

Wen thought of Shu Ling wearing the sparkly jersey. Shu Ling would pivot slowly on her good leg and say, "Look at me, *mei mei*, in my new shirt. Don't I look just like a princess?"

Wen felt an unexpected warmth toward her mother. She wanted tell her mother how grateful she was, but she couldn't.

"Shu Ling says 'thank you,'" Wen said instead. "You make Shu Ling much happy."

Back home, Wen spread out Shu Ling's new clothes on the sofa to admire them side by side.

"Hi, Mom!" Emily greeted her mother, who'd just come in carrying the last shopping bag.

How easily Emily said it. Mom. *Hi, Mom,* Wen wished she could say. But whenever she opened her mouth to say *Mom,* the word stuck in her throat. The aunties taught kids picked for adoption to call their mothers *Mama.* But all Wen could do was call her mother *Hey.*

"Let's show Wennie our family album," said Emily.

"The photos! Great idea." Wen's mother pulled out

a thick book from a shelf under a table. Carefully, they folded up Shu Ling's shirts and sat on the sofa, Wen in the middle. Her mother set the heavy book on Wen's lap.

"Where should we start? How about with Grandma Jackson?" With her fingertips, Wen's mother traced a tall slender woman with a gaunt face and bright blue eyes. "Here's my mother, Wen. Your grandmother. She can't wait to meet you."

Her mother had her own mother. Wen hadn't thought of that.

"Here you are, Wennie. This was the first picture we got of you." Emily flipped toward the end of the book.

Wen saw a tiny picture of her, in the common room, her hair pulled back in high pigtails, a little half-moon smile spread across her cheeks.

Wen flipped back to the earlier pages. She came to a baby with jet-black hair, snuggled against her mother, her father beaming right beside them. "Emily!" she said.

"Yes, that's right at the orphanage, the day we adopted Emily," her mother said.

"You were baby!" Wen said. Of course. She should have known.

"We loved having our baby, Emily. And then we wanted an older girl." Her mother looked straight at Wen. "That's why we picked you."

No wonder it was easy for Emily to call her mother Mom and let her hug her and kiss her good night. Emily had been here so long.

Wen saw snapshots of Emily learning how to walk. She saw Emily in fuzzy PJs, fast asleep in her mother's arms.

*What else did I miss?* Wen wondered.

"See, here's me at my first birthday, Wennie." Emily showed her a little girl sitting in front of a cake with one lit candle, frosting spread all over her face.

"You could be a handful at that age, Em!" Her mother laughed.

So they didn't send Emily back when she wasn't perfect.

But Emily had been so little, Wen reminded herself. Things were different for her. Wen was older, so she had no excuse for behaving badly. She still had to be very, very good.

When would she see the keeping sign? Until she did, she couldn't ask about Shu Ling, who might get some new shirts but still needed a family more than anything else.

# ten

After she sent Shu Ling her letter and the shirts, Wen began sorting the mail every day after school. Yet weeks passed and still no letter came from Shu Ling.

Why wasn't Shu Ling writing back? Had the phone call made Shu Ling so sad she couldn't even get up, like the time with the new baby?

Last year, Shu Ling had taken special care of a new baby girl who'd been found at a train station, wrapped in tissue paper. She swaddled the frail baby in a pale yellow blanket and named her Xiao Dan, which meant "Little Dawn." When feeding time was over, Wen watched Shu Ling cooing soft lullabies as she rocked tiny Xiao Dan in her arms. The baby would lift her sunken dark eyes to Shu Ling and give her a tiny wisp of a smile.

One day, Wen went with Shu Ling to Xiao Dan's crib. It was empty. "Where's the baby?" Shu Ling had screamed. Auntie Min said she'd died in the night. Sobbing, Shu Ling clung to the yellow blanket, all she had left of her Xiao Dan.

Shu Ling stayed in bed for two weeks, too weak to

move. Finally, Wen pulled her from her cot, angled her shoulder so Shu Ling's arm would fit, and made her walk to breakfast.

Was Shu Ling so sad now she was staying in bed all day long? Or had she gotten in trouble, like maybe for not doing her chores?

Every day, Wen rifled through catalogues and envelopes. Every day there was no letter from Shu Ling.

At school, Wen tried to concentrate, when she really wanted to run home to see if a letter from Shu Ling had arrived yet. One Tuesday, the kids made invitations for the parents' breakfast, which was coming up at the end of October. Ms. Beckwith led the class into the computer lab and assigned everybody to groups. She put Wen with Hannah.

"Wen, do you know how to use a computer?" Hannah asked.

"Little bit," Wen said. At the orphanage school, the computer screen went blank one day. Teacher Jun shook and banged the monitor, but still the screen stayed dark. So Teacher Jun had lugged the computer to the gully. From the windows, the kids cheered as he hurled the old computer into the pit, where it landed on a rock and smashed into a spray of silvery splinters.

Hannah taught Wen how to find alphabet letters on the keyboard until Wen had printed out a perfect invitation.

PLEASE COME! BREAKFAST!
FRIDAY, 29th Day of October
7:30 MUCH FOOD

When she got home from school that afternoon, Wen kept the invitation tucked in her backpack. Should she show her parents? Would they even want to come? Maybe they'd feel she was asking too much. She couldn't risk that.

Then she saw the mail, still on the floor. Wen knelt beside the letters and catalogs, her fingers frantic.

A letter from Shu Ling! Wen tore open the front flap.

Dear Mei Mei,

Your letter made me so happy! Your plan is good, mei mei. Auntie Lan Lan reminds us about An Fei all the time. Mainly, I think you have to show your family how grateful you are that they chose you.

I can't believe we'll really be together in the same family. I feel like I already know your father, Round Man, your mother with the sunshine hair, and cute Emily! When you ask, be sure to tell them I am good at chores and I could cook noodles every night.

Oh, and thank you for the beautiful shirts. Auntie
Mu Hong put them in the common wardrobe. There
was nothing to be done. I liked the shirt with the
sparkles best.

Lu Li and Tai both got adopted yesterday. I helped
Lu Li get ready. She was a little shy, so I said, just like
Auntie Lan Lan, This is your lucky day, and then she
even laughed. The aunties dressed Tai in the sparkly
jersey you sent me, mei mei, so she would look her
best for her new family. She was very beautiful in that
shirt but I couldn't watch her for too long.

Shan and Mei Lin turned eighteen, so they went
to the village up north, for jobs at the coal mining
plant. Now it is only me in our row and Yu Ming, who
is still very mean. The rest are the little girls. Auntie
Lan Lan said more older girls are coming next week,
from the hospital.

Write me back about how your plan is going.

Love,

Shu Ling

P.S. I am sending along a picture one of the adoptive
parents took of me. See, I am wearing your bright red
tunic. I know you picked the red for good luck!


Wen  reread  the  letter,  then  folded  it  back  in  the

envelope, along with Shu Ling's photo. She stuffed the thick packet into her chest pocket, to keep her strong as she waited for the sign that her parents would keep her forever.

ℓℓ

"Guess what's coming, Wennie? Halloween!" Emily announced later that week.

"What is this *Hall-oh-een?*" asked Wen. "A festival?"

"Festival?" Emily stopped to stare at Wen. "Well, yeah, you could say it's a festival. I guess you don't have Halloween in China, right?"

"This festival we do not have."

"On Halloween, kids get dressed up and trick-or-treat. I'm going as a cat." Emily curved her hands like paws and purred. "Anyway, we go trick-or-treating and get lots of free candy."

"Candy for free! This I cannot believe!" Wen opened her eyes wide.

"Much as you want," Emily said. She licked her lips. "Yummy!"

"Jolly Ranchers?" Wen asked. Shu Ling loved Jolly Ranchers. Maybe she could go to the Halloween festival and get lots of Jolly Ranchers to send to Shu Ling as a surprise.

When the American parents had come to the orphanage with candy, the aunties made the children line up so they could each pick a piece. Everybody pushed and squabbled to get to the front first.

"Don't wait for me," Shu Ling would call. They both knew her leg would slow her down. So Wen would get in line and, if she was lucky, scoop up a package of Jolly Ranchers. She'd return to Shu Ling, carrying her prize.

"Oh, *mei mei*, you did it," Shu Ling would say. "My very favorite candy!"

"Jolly Ranchers?" Emily repeated, now. "I guess. If that's what you like. What are you going to be, Wennie?"

"Be?"

"Kids wear costumes. Funny clothes, for trick-or-treating. You'll love Halloween, Wen!" Emily whooped.

Just then, Wen's mother came through the front door and dumped bamboo-shaped rolls, like paper towel holders, on the kitchen table.

"Mom, you are back to the architecting again?" Emily asked.

Wen's mother nodded. "They're even letting me work from home lots of days."

"What is this architecting?" Wen asked.

"Means she makes maps of houses on big papers with a ruler. Right, Mom?" Emily asked.

Wen's mother laughed. "Right. So girls, how was school

today?"

With her toe, Wen kicked her backpack under the kitchen table.

Should she show her mother the breakfast invitation after all? Maybe her mother would be mad because she had something else more important to do, like this architecting. But suppose her mother really wanted to go? Then she'd be angry if Wen didn't invite her.

Wen pulled out the folded piece of paper. "Have something. Made this for you but you could forget it."

Her mother read the paper. "This is great, Wen. A parent breakfast!"

"OK if you not go. Maybe Dad already at work. Maybe you too busy making house maps," Wen said.

"Of course we'll be there." Then her mother looked her in the eyes. "Remember, we're your parents, Wen, and we'd love to come. We'll come to all your class breakfasts and your class plays and science fairs. When you move from sixth grade to middle school next fall, we'll go to everything you invite us to," her mother went on. "We'll go to your graduation from middle school and we'll chaperone your high school prom, if you let us. We'll be there with bells on for your high school graduation and we'll cheer at your college graduation. If you decide to get married, we'll sit in the front row at your wedding, and if you have children, we'll bounce them on our knee and spoil them rotten!" Her mother swept her arms through the air, as if she were gathering up Wen's life, right in front of her.

Wen felt a flash of recognition, a stirring of joy that made her want to dance and scream out loud. Wen knew what her mother's words were.

*The keeping sign, at last!*

# eleven

"Wennie, save me a doughnut, OK?" said Emily, sitting in the backseat with Wen. Wen's father had offered to drive the whole family to school on the day of the parent breakfast.

"What is this *doh-nut?*"

"Food. Big circle with hole." Emily arched both hands over her head.

Suppose she got caught, like the time at home with the muffin and the banana? Suppose she got in a lot of trouble, just when her parents had decided to keep her? And all because of Emily.

"Maybe," Wen said. "If possible."

On the way to school, Wen thought about how this breakfast had led to the sign, and now she could ask her parents to adopt Shu Ling.

Of course they'd say yes. They had to. But just to be sure, Wen decided she'd bring it up next Wednesday, at her father's birthday dinner. Her mother, Emily, and she had already planned out the party. Everybody would be there; nobody could be late. Emily had asked her father to bring home pepperoni pizza—for no reason special, Emily had told him, winking at Wen. Wen and Emily would bake a chocolate birthday cake, frosted with chocolate icing and lots of sprinkles. Her mother was picking up her dad's favorite ice cream, Moose Tracks. Everybody would be in a good mood at this wonderful birthday party. It would be the perfect time to ask about Shu Ling.

After the last of the ice cream, Wen would say, *I have a friend who needs a home. Can you adopt her, too?*

And she could almost see her mother nodding, saying there was always room for one more, there was plenty of love to go around. She could hear her father asking if Shu Ling liked bacon.

*ℓℓ*

As Wen and her parents walked into the classroom, Wen wanted to put her hands over her ears. People were chattering in English so fast they seemed to be spitting out their words.

"Hi, Christine!" A woman wearing a butter-colored jacket rushed up to her mother and hugged her.

"Oh, Susan, it's been an age!" Wen's mother and the other lady held on to each other for what seemed to Wen a long time.

Unexpectedly, Wen felt an ache that had nothing to do with skipping breakfast at home that morning. She longed to hug her mother that way too. Something always made her hold back.

"Hey, let's get some of that food." Wen's father led her toward a long table where bread slices, muffins, and circles with holes were arranged on plates. But Wen moved toward the windows to get away from all the people whose English seemed to get louder and louder.

In front of her, she saw Hannah and Michelle. Hannah was gazing out the window, toward the school parking lot, while, beside her, Michelle munched on a muffin.

"He said he'd come," Wen heard Hannah say, twisting the silver ring on her littlest finger.

"Hannah, your father never shows up. Period. Don't waste your time." Michelle rolled her eyes.

"He promised!" Hannah wailed. "He knew Mom had to work, so he said he'd be here!"

"So what else is new? I'm going to get some orange juice." Michelle steered through the crowd.

Very quietly, Wen took a step and stood beside Hannah. She watched the parking lot too. Maybe if the two of them stared very hard, they could see the car better when it came.

"What color is car?" Wen asked.

"Wen!" Hannah turned to her. "I didn't see you there."

"You are looking for someone." Wen kept her eyes focused on the parking lot.

"It's my dad. He's late," Hannah told her. "His car is red."

"I help you look."

"Thanks." Hannah smiled at Wen and then returned her eyes to the window.

"He gave you the beautiful ring?" Wen asked.

"How did you know? See, it's a special present!" Hannah held up her little finger to show Wen the tiny ring.

"Ring is nice. And your father, he is many times late?" asked Wen.

"Well, actually, he usually just never comes at all," Hannah said flatly.

"You miss him greatly," said Wen. "You not see him much?"

"They're divorced."

Wen tilted her head. What was this *di-vorce* Hannah spoke of?

"Divorced. Split up." Hannah put her arms together across her chest then thrust them apart.

Divided, like pieces of an orange, Wen decided.

"Di-vorced long time?" Wen hoped she had said this new word right.

"Since last August. My dad lives in Rhode Island now. I miss him so much!"

"He was in your life, now nothing," Wen said.

Turning toward Wen, Hannah blinked. "You get it. You actually get it."

"This missing, I know."

Hannah took her eyes off the parking lot and studied

Wen as if she were just now seeing her. "Of course you do. You must miss your friends back in China."

Wen nodded, gazing at the parking lot as if she, too, were searching for someone she knew. "Have good friend there, her name is Shu Ling. Miss her greatly."

Just then, Ms. Beckwith clapped her hands for silence and thanked the parents for coming. After the parents left, Wen and Hannah went to their desks.

"Hey, Wen," Hannah said. "Do you want to come trick-or-treating with us on Halloween? It's Sunday night."

"Halloween," Wen repeated, relieved that she knew what Hannah was talking about.

"Right. We're meeting at my house to get dressed around six. Just wear something black, OK? And sunglasses and boots, if you have them. We're going as a rock band."

Wen thought of all the Jolly Ranchers she could get for Shu Ling. Then, despite herself, she thought about all the new candy she wanted to taste for herself.

"I come," said Wen.

# twelve

At six o'clock on Halloween, Wen and her mother drove over to Hannah's house, across town. While the mothers chatted, Hannah took Wen's arm.

"C'mon," she said. "We're in the bathroom, getting ready."

Michelle poked her head out of the bathroom.

"Have fun, sweetie," Wen's mother called. "I'll come back for you around ten."

"Bye." Wen caught a final glimpse of her mother leaving.

"That was your mom?" Michelle asked. "She's American. So that must mean you're *adopted*, right?"

"You're adopted, Wen! That's cool." Hannah put her arm around Wen.

"What happened to your real parents?" Michelle demanded.

Wen felt like she was being exposed, the way Cook would tear skin off a chicken to reveal the raw meat beneath. She couldn't even begin to reply.

"Jeez, could you be any nosier, Michelle?" Hannah turned to Wen. "You know you don't have to answer that, right?"

Wen gave Hannah a grateful smile.

Hannah steered Wen into the bathroom. "Don't let Michelle get to you," she whispered. "She's changed a lot lately."

"Say such mean things." Twisting her head, Wen checked behind her, to be sure she was far enough away from Michelle.

"I know." Hannah put her arm around Wen's neck. "Try to stick up for yourself. Or I will."

By the sink, Sophie was spraying her hair bright blue.

"Hey, Wen!" Sophie put down her can. "Do you want your hair neon blue, orange, or metallic gold? Don't worry, it washes off; it's not permanent or anything."

"Orange," said Wen. She covered her face with a towel while Sophie sprayed her hair a bright orange. Her clumps of hair, now longer, lay flat and glistened like the freshly washed tangerines the aunties passed out at Lunar New Year. In the mirror, Wen could barely recognize herself. She was beautiful.

Then she thought of Shu Ling. Maybe Shu Ling would be here next year. What color hair would she pick? She might be best in the glittery gold.

"How will people know we're a rock band?" Michelle spiked her neon blue bangs with gel.

"Because we look cool and our hair's weird, that's how," said Hannah, smearing her lids with black eye shadow. "Want some?" she asked Wen.

Wen closed her eyes while Hannah gently smoothed waxy black cream on her eyelids. Next year she'd put the cream on Shu Ling's big eyes. Then they'd stand together in the mirror and Wen would admire Shu Ling's golden hair and blacked eyelids. *You're just like a movie star,* she'd say.

*So are you,* mei mei, Shu Ling would answer.

Now, through her orange bangs, Wen saw Sophie standing on the vanity chair. "Time to go," Sophie announced. "Don't forget your sunglasses."

"But it's dark out and we won't be able to see!" Michelle complained.

"Seriously, we'd better get going or we'll miss out on the good candy," Sophie said. "Here, grab a pillowcase. I brought four."

A pillowcase? That much candy? Wen took her pillowcase and followed the others.

"So you just ring the doorbell, nothing to it," Hannah explained, wobbling on her high-heeled boots. "Then they give you candy and you're off to the next house."

Wen walked beside the others as they went from house to house, ringing doorbells and saying trick-or-treat. They walked so slowly, Wen knew Shu Ling would be able to keep up.

After a while, Wen's bag got heavy and she had to lug it with both hands.

"Let's go back to my house and count our loot," said Hannah.

Back at Hannah's, the girls sat on the kitchen floor. They turned their pillowcases inside out and spilled mountains of candy in front of them. Wen saw little cups covered in orange foil, long sticks wrapped in blue, round candy on sticks, and tiny chocolate-colored envelopes.

Wen had never seen so much candy. In her own mound, she spotted Snickers, Tootsie Roll Pops, and lots of Jolly Ranchers.

"What's your favorite kind of candy, Wen?" asked Hannah.

"Don't know." Wen gaped at the huge pile.

"Maybe they don't have candy like this in China," Sophie said.

"M&M's, yes," Wen said. "Not these many."

"Hey, Michelle, let Wen try your Reese's," said Hannah.

"Fine. Take it then." Michelle pushed the candy across the floor in Wen's direction and began busily stacking up her Almond Joys.

Wen eyed Michelle, her red-lipsticked mouth pouting, her slender body hunched over, guarding her candy. Then Wen thought of Shu Ling, how her eyes would sparkle in delight at all the candy heaped in front of Michelle.

"Thanks, Michelle," Wen said coolly.

*Spoiled brat*, she added, to herself.

Very carefully, Wen picked up the Reese's, peeled off the foil, and undid the pleated brown paper around the tiny candy, shaped like one of her mother's muffins. She bit into the Reese's and felt the smooth peanut butter and chocolate melt on her tongue.

"Ohhh," whispered Wen. She closed her eyes. "Oh!"

"If she likes Reese's, give her a Twix!" Hannah offered her a rectangular-shaped candy with bright red letters across the top. "Wen, try this!"

Wen ripped open the coppery wrapper and bit into the candy. This one crunched, as she tasted a sweet rush of cookies, chocolate, and caramel.

"Try an Almond Joy, Wen." From across the floor, Sophie shot a blue package her way. Now she knew how to rip open the shiny paper quickly. Wen nibbled on the oval chocolate piece and discovered a new kind of sweetness.

"What this taste?" she asked.

"Coconut. Now keep going," urged Sophie.

Then she crunched into a nut.

"That's the almond part of the joy, Wen!" Hannah laughed.

Wen felt the chocolate, coconut, and almond flavors blend in her mouth. She grinned. "What try next?"

"OK, tasting's over; time for trades. I'm sure Wen gets the idea by now," said Michelle.

Wen wanted to keep on tasting. Frowning at Michelle, she felt the sweetness in her mouth turn sour.

"Trades," Michelle repeated. "Who'll give me Snickers or Hershey bars for all my Almond Joys?"

"You don't like Almond Joys, Michelle? Are you nuts?"

Sophie tossed over three Snickers and took back a handful of Michelle's Almond Joys.

"Twizzlers," Hannah announced. "What do I get for ten Twizzlers?"

Sophie tossed six Tootsie Roll Pops and pocketed Hannah's Twizzlers.

"Jolly Ranchers," said Wen. "I present you all my candy. You give me your Jolly Ranchers, your cherry, your strawberry, and your grape—any kind. Just want Jolly Ranchers." With one arm, she moved her mountain of candy to the center of the table.

"Ah, Wen . . ." Hannah nudged her. "That's not such a great deal," she muttered.

"This I do," said Wen. "Give all Jolly Ranchers, take this whole ton."

"Wen, you can't just give away all your candy, your whole night's candy, for a few crummy Jolly Ranchers," Hannah said.

"It OK." Wen dropped the little candies into her pillowcase. "Love Jolly Ranchers."

In the end, Wen got forty-four Jolly Ranchers.

As she dumped the Jolly Ranchers into her sack, she thought about how she'd mail them to Shu Ling in big envelopes, each neatly padded with a layer of Jolly Ranchers. If Auntie Lan Lan gave out the mail, maybe she would figure out the Jolly Ranchers but let Shu Ling have them for herself. Wen pictured Shu Ling choosing a different flavor of Jolly Rancher every night.

Better yet, Shu Ling would get her own Jolly Ranchers when she came trick-or-treating next year.

Wen heard her mother at the door.

Hannah tossed some Reese's and Almond Joys into Wen's bag. "You've got to have more than Jolly Ranchers on your first Halloween in America," Hannah said.

"Thanks for inviting me to this trick-or-treat festival," Wen said.

"We'll do it again next year," Hannah said.

In the car, Wen held Shu Ling's Jolly Ranchers close to her chest. Nearing home, as she gulped the last morsel of Hannah's candy, Wen's stomach began to feel queasy. Then she thought of her father's birthday, just three days away. Very soon, she'd be raising the question she'd waited for so long to ask.

The time had come to say to her family: *Will you adopt Shu Ling?*

# thirteen

On Wednesday evening, Wen sat on the kitchen chair nearest the door, waiting for the sound of her father's car in the driveway. Tonight was the night.

Wen's throat felt scratchy. She clutched and unclutched her sweaty hands.

Finally she heard the car and then her father's footsteps on the porch.

She decided she couldn't wait until after the ice cream. As soon as they'd divided up the gooey pizza, she'd tell them all about Shu Ling and why she needed a family too. At last, she could ask! Wen imagined herself bursting with happiness when they said yes.

Then she saw her father come in. He walked stiffly, and his arms were empty.

"What's wrong, Richard?" Her mother dried her hands and went to him.

Wen noticed her father's usually rosy skin was pale and his eyes were drawn.

"Oh, Christine . . ." His coat still on, he sat down in a kitchen chair.

"Daddy, what's up?" Emily asked.

Gripping a saltshaker, Wen's father gazed at her mother, at Emily, and at her, one by one. "I got laid off," he announced, his voice so shaky Wen thought he might cry.

"Oh, no!" Her mother sat down next to her father and put her hand on his arm.

*"Laid off"... what did this mean?* Wen wondered. *It must be something very bad.*

"Christine, it came from nowhere," her father said.

Wen heard the rawness in his voice as he huddled in his buttoned-up coat. Her father seemed smaller, as if he were shrunken by whatever the laid off had done.

"So what happened, exactly?" her mother asked.

"Well, revenue was down, we all knew that," he began.

"But nobody was talking about layoffs, right?" her mother asked.

"Not then, they weren't. Today around four, my boss called me in and he said, 'Rich, this had nothing to do with you personally, but Central Office says we have to cut fifty employees and even though you're a top manager, I have to let you go.'"

Wen strained to understand. Then with amazement, Wen saw her father set down the saltshaker and put his face in his hands.

*He thinks he's done something wrong,* she thought.

"So, when's your last day of work, Richard?" Wen heard

her mother's voice coming from someplace deep, like she was speaking from a pit.

"Today. He gave me one hour to clear out my office and get out." Her father's voice wavered.

Now Wen got it. He had to leave his job.

Only then did Wen fully realize what had just happened. She couldn't ask them to adopt Shu Ling tonight, or any other time, as long as her father had no job.

Why hadn't she asked earlier, as soon as she got the sign from her mother? She should have asked then, on the ride to the parent breakfast. Her parents would have agreed, back then, when her father was working. Why did she think her father's birthday party was so important? Just because everybody in the whole family would be there? Just because they'd all be in a good mood? Why did she think she needed such a perfect way of asking? She shouldn't have wasted time!

Now, because of her, Shu Ling had no hope of a family. It was all her fault.

*"Today* was your last day?" Wen's mother said. "I can't believe it! And no notice?"

"Well, I can collect unemployment, of course."

"Daddy, you don't have a job anymore?" Emily sat down beside him and Wen took the other chair. It was odd to be sitting together in the kitchen, no places set, nobody eating. Her father stared at the table, her mother was digging her fingernails into her palms, and Emily sat still, not even squirming.

"Of course I'll start looking right away. Hiring may be slow over the holidays," her father said. "But I'm sure to find something."

"What is this hiring?" Wen saw her father's forehead drawn, and new lines around his eyes. He seemed to slouch a little, as if his back hurt.

"It means getting a job," her father said, his voice flat.

Nobody spoke.

Then her mother cleared her throat. "OK. We need a plan."

"The plan is, I'm unemployed, Christine," her father snapped.

"We have to make it work, that's all," her mother said, with that firmness she took when she expected no arguing. "Richard, you're bound to find new work soon and I can take on some extra projects with the firm."

Her mother filled a pot of water and boiled pasta for dinner.

"None for me, Chris," said her father.

One day after dinner the following week, Wen's father cleared his throat. "Mom and I thought we should have a family talk," he began.

"We wanted you girls to know that since Dad's not working right now, we're going to have to start cutting back on extras," Wen's mother said.

*Extras?* Wen felt like she'd been cracked across the chest, her breath escaping her.

*I just got here,* Wen thought. *Am I an extra? Of course I'm an extra. They did fine without me before, for a long time. They can do fine without me now.*

"Does this mean we can't go to the *mall* anymore?" Emily wailed.

"It does, honey," her mother answered.

"But I love our trips to the mall! How can we not go to the mall?" Emily whined.

As she gazed at Emily, Wen couldn't help thinking of all the kids at the orphanage who'd never even heard of a mall.

"Emily, you can live without the mall!" her father exploded.

"What other extras?" Emily demanded.

"Well, we've decided to trade in your mother's new car for a used one," said her father.

"And Emily, I'm afraid we'll have to put your gymnastics on hold for a while." Her mother reached to hug Emily.

"It's not fair!" Emily stamped her foot.

"Sweetie, gymnastics costs a lot of money. You can start again once Dad gets a job."

"But I love gymnastics! I'm starting to work on the balance beams, Mom!" Emily wailed. "What'll I do without gymnastics? It's not like I can play with *her*." Emily pointed at Wen.

So far the extras had mainly hit Emily. But the real extra, Wen knew, was herself.

After she cleared the table, Wen pulled on her hoodie and went outside to sit on the porch steps.

Wen heard her parents at the table, still talking, their voices low. In the living room, Emily sat in the old rocking chair. The rocker squeaked as Emily moved.

Then Wen heard another squeaking, from years ago, when she was five. She remembered for the first time.

Her mother had been sitting on the wooden rocker, nursing Wen's new baby brother, in the one room of their hut, where everybody ate and slept. As her rocker squeaked, her mother had told Wen to go outside because the grown-ups needed to talk. Wen obeyed, but stayed by an open window so she could hear.

Her father had said the drought had been too long, the crops were failing. They had to leave the farm. Otherwise, he warned, the whole family would starve. Then Wen heard more squeaking from the rocker, and her mother asked where they'd go.

Her father talked about his uncle's apartment in the city. It had a spare room large enough for three people. They'd take their new son.

"What about Wen?" her mother asked.

An extra, her father had said. Besides, in cities, extra girls were against the law.

"Not Wen. Not my daughter!" Wen's mother pleaded. "Not my little girl!" She sobbed and then her sobbing turned to wails.

It was settled, her father said.

The next day, her mother took her by the hand and walked her to the crumbling pink building on the hill.

Now, just when she thought she'd found a family that would keep her, Wen was an extra all over again.

The squeaking inside had stopped. Wen got up from the porch and went into her room. She pulled out her old orphanage backpack so she'd be all ready for when they told her it was time to go back.

<hr>

"Brrrr, it's cold in here," Emily said the next day. She made her teeth chatter as she put on a second sweatshirt.

"Oil's expensive this winter. We're turning down the thermostat," said her father.

Wen had noticed. Of course, it wasn't as cold as the orphanage. But she'd begun to wear layers, just as she had when the aunties turned the furnace on for four hours in the morning and then shut it down for the rest of the day, to save coal.

On Saturday morning, their father made them stacks of

steamy pancakes, which stood out, lonely, on the breakfast plates.

Another extra to go: *bacon*.

After breakfast, Wen peered through her father's partly opened study door. Sipping coffee from a cracked cup, he stared at his computer screen. Sometimes he stopped and examined the ceiling or stretched his fingers as if to loosen them.

"Wen!" her father said. "I didn't see you there."

"Have something for you." She waved a wad of dollar bills. "My monies."

"That's your allowance, Wen."

"Monies we need right now. I not spend anyway."

"No, you keep that, sweetie."

"You look hard on computer. This computer has jobs for hiring?" Wen asked.

"Yes, it does. Certain Web sites, Wen. Plus I'm talking to people I know." Her father spoke in a cheerful voice Wen knew was forced.

"You get a job maybe next week?" Wen asked.

He had to find a job soon, so she wouldn't be an extra and she could ask about Shu Ling.

"Oh no, honey. I don't think so. It may just take some time, that's all. There's no need to worry, Wen," her father said.

"I not worry. You not worry, either, Dad." Wen held up the crossed-fingers sign. "You get job any day now."

Her father grinned and held up his own crossed fingers. "Thanks, Wen."

Back in her room, Wen flexed her hand. Maybe even crossing fingers wouldn't help.

Until she got sent back, Wen knew she had to spend every day in America finding Shu Ling a family of her own. It couldn't be her own family anymore. She'd have to find some other nice family to adopt Shu Ling. But who else could she ask?

She could call kids in her class. Ms. Beckwith had passed out little books with the phone numbers of all the families in the school. But when Wen thought of calling those kids, she winced. How could she tell them about her friend as close as a sister, a friend she had failed? She couldn't reveal herself that way.

Where were some happy families that might adopt a new daughter?

Suddenly, Wen had an idea.

# fourteen

Happy families went to McDonald's. Wen had decided that she'd find a happy family right there and tell them all about Shu Ling.

But how could she do this? How could she talk to people whom she didn't even know? Her English might disappear, talking to strangers.

She'd make an invitation, like for the parent breakfast—that was it! Only this would be an invitation to adopt Shu Ling, an invitation she could give to all those families.

At the kitchen computer the next afternoon, Wen hunted and clicked the right alphabet keys.

**Want a daughter? This nice girl needs family.**
**She waits for you!**

But what would the family do, if they wanted to adopt Shu Ling? From the bulletin board, Wen unpinned Nancy Lin's phone number and copied it onto the sheets.

"Dad," she called to her father, sliding the flyers into her parka, "I go on walk."

"Just a short one, Wen," her father said.

"Back soon!" It was so cold, Wen could see her breath, like puffs of mist as she walked along the edge of the highway. After a long time, she came to the bright yellow arches.

Her legs aching, Wen headed toward the entrance. First she had to pick a family that looked good and then hand them an invitation. *Tell us about this nice girl*, they would say. And Wen had to hope she could form the English to tell them how Shu Ling was a big help, did chores, cooked soup, and drew beautiful pictures.

Her legs shaking, Wen planted herself at the front door. *Must do this*, she told herself.

A mother and her daughter came first, the little girl screaming and tugging on her mother's arm. Swearing, the mother yanked the little girl behind her.

*Not a good family*, Wen decided.

Then came a mother and father swinging a little boy between them. They were all laughing, their cheeks rosy from the cold.

Walking toward the parents, Wen offered the mother a flyer. "Something to tell you," she began, her voice hoarse. But the lady stuffed the flyer into her pocket, kept swinging the boy, and ignored her.

A man entered, carrying a sobbing boy in his arms. The father seemed desperate for help. "Here, maybe your son need big sister," Wen said, trying to comfort the man with a soothing voice. She handed him an invitation. He thanked her, then hurried toward the counter, the boy still wailing.

Next, a bunch of girls all dressed in shiny blue shorts and shirts with numbers on their backs surged past Wen.

"Fries!" screamed a tall girl, her eyes fixed on the counter ahead.

"Wait for us!" shouted another girl as she shoved past Wen. Clutching her flyers, Wen teetered and smashed her knee against the railing. She grabbed the trash can to steady herself.

Wen stared into the trash, piled high with wet cups and greasy plates. All around her, Wen heard screaming English she didn't understand, so loud her ears rang. Her knee hurt. Wen edged toward the door, crushed her flyers to her chest, and zipped up her parka.

Then, very slowly, she limped home, making a *stomp-drag* all the way.

~ll~

Her parents were waiting on the porch. Wen saw her mother, paler than usual, gripping a railing, as if to support herself. Her father paced from one stair to another, his eyes scanning the street.

"Wen! Oh, thank God!" Her mother seemed to collapse in relief.

"Where were you, Wen?" her father demanded.

"Walk. Remember? I told you this," Wen answered, lowering her eyes.

"You said 'short,' Wen!" her father shouted. "You were gone over three hours."

"We found your cell phone here, so we couldn't call," her mother accused. Little creases fanned around her brow.

"You were gone so long, we thought something had happened, Wen," her father said.

"Where were you, Wen? Were you running away?" her mother asked.

"I not run away," Wen said.

They were so angry. Now they'd change their minds and send her back as an extra for sure.

"We have to know, Wen. We're your parents and we need to know where you go." Her mother waited for an answer.

Wen froze. What should she tell them? She was trying to find a home for Shu Ling, all on her own, keeping a secret from them. That might make her parents mad, like she wasn't even grateful for the home they gave her.

"Wen, if you can't tell us, you'll have to stay in your room until you're ready. You owe us an explanation," her father said.

She had to tell the whole story. No matter what happened.

"OK. My friend Shu Ling," Wen began. "Shu Ling wait too long in orphanage. She need own family here in

America. I made big promise." Wen met her mother's gaze. "I told her, she come next. I find her a family too. But this I cannot do. Not know how. I went to the McDonald's, for family. This not work well."

"McDonald's? Is that where you were, Wen? That's so far away." Wen's mother shuddered.

"Only way I could do," said Wen. "Had to do this."

"But why didn't you ask us for help, Wen?" her father asked.

"I could not."

"All these weeks here and you couldn't just say, 'I want to get a home for Shu Ling'? Why not?" her mother asked.

"Afraid," Wen whispered.

"Afraid of what? Tell us, Wen," her mother said.

Wen hesitated. "Afraid," she began, her voice low. "Afraid you send me back for asking for too much."

"Send you back? Where did you get that idea?" her mother asked.

"This happened to An Fei."

"Oh, Wen." Wen's mother sighed. "You're family. We would never send you back. You belong with us."

"But now Dad has no job," Wen said. "So I think, maybe I'm an extra, you cut me out."

"Nobody's an extra in a family, Wen." As if she couldn't help herself, her mother gave her a quick hug.

Wen felt numb. "Not an extra," she repeated.

"Never an extra," her mother stated firmly. "Never."

"Here, you must be thirsty after that McDonald's hike. Let's go inside and get you something to drink," her father said.

As Wen sipped her water, she kept repeating her parents' words in her mind, as if to memorize them. Then she went back to her bedroom and picked up the old orphanage backpack waiting in the front of her closet. She flung the whole backpack where it had come from, in a dark, unused corner. She wouldn't need it after all.

Wen returned to the kitchen. "So about Shu Ling. This is possible, find her a family?"

"We can help you," said her mother. "After all, we found you, didn't we?"

"How we do this?" Wen asked.

Carefully, her mother explained how the directors of the orphanages were allowed to send the Chinese government a certain number of names of kids available for adoption. Then the government added those names to the Shared Waiting Child List for families from all over the world to choose from.

"Why just pick some? Every single kid in orphanage should be available for adoption. All just waiting for the day a family come to take them home."

"I know, sweetie," her mother sighed. "That's just how they do it."

"Many kids on The List?" Wen asked.

"Over two thousand and counting," her mother said.

Wen swallowed. "Is Shu Ling on The List?"

"We don't know. Only adoption agency people have the password to that list. Nancy will know."

"We call Nancy now!" Wen pleaded.

"It's Sunday, sweetie. You can call tomorrow."

Wen felt like tomorrow would never come. If Shu Ling wasn't on The List, it would be impossible for anyone to adopt her. She had to be there.

But suppose she wasn't?

# fifteen

"You can call Nancy the minute you get home from school," Wen's mother assured her.

But how could she go a whole day not knowing if Shu Ling was on The List?

At the bus stop, Wen watched Emily and another girl catching snowflakes on their tongues. Two boys beside them were trying to scoop up enough snow for snowballs.

"Hi, Wen," she heard a voice say behind her.

"Hannah!" Wen said. She waited to see Hannah's sparkly teeth, but Hannah wasn't smiling. "Why you are on our bus, not your own?"

"From now on, this is my bus." Hannah's blue eyes were clouded just like they'd been at the parent breakfast.

"Something is wrong?" Wen asked.

Hannah shivered.

"Maybe you take this bus just one day?" Wen tried.

"My mom and I moved," Hannah said. "To a smaller house."

"But you will still see your father?" Wen said.

"Yes. But I can't help it, Wen. I just can't get used to this divorce. I still miss him. And the new house makes it more real that he's not coming home."

"Like it used to be," Wen said. "Of course."

When the bus came, everybody filed in the door, the boys shoving last. Hannah and Wen sat together in the back.

"Michelle says half of the kids in America have divorced parents." Hannah sighed. "She says it's bad but it's not such a big deal."

"Big deal for you. You still miss your father."

Hannah's eyes filled with tears. "I really miss him."

Wen nodded. "This I know."

"Is it hard for you, too, Wen? Missing your friends from China?" Hannah asked.

"Yes. Just learned Shu Ling may be on Big List, ready to go for adoption in this country. Learned yesterday."

"Well, that's great!" Hannah smiled a little, but not enough for her starry teeth to show.

"But maybe she is not on this list. Don't know yet." Wen sighed.

"Oh, no. Then you'd still have to miss her," Hannah said.

"That's it," Wen said.

Hannah lowered her voice. "There's something I've been meaning to tell you, Wen. About Michelle."

"She says many mean things," Wen blurted.

"I know. She and I have been friends since first grade. But when the divorce happened, she just acted like it was no big deal. Basically, she said 'Suck it up.'"

"'Suck it up'?" Wen repeated.

"It's like saying forget about it," Hannah explained. "So because of that, since last summer I haven't been hanging out with her as much. I think maybe she's a little bit jealous of you, Wen."

"Why jealous of me?" Wen's eyes widened.

"She gets jealous easy. Seriously. Back when I was in third grade, my family hosted a Chinese foreign exchange student. I really liked her, and I lived with her, for heaven's sake. But Michelle got really jealous. So I think when she heard you were coming, from China and all, she got jealous of you even before she met you!"

Wen paused. "Maybe Michelle not like China people."

"No. She just always wants me to be her best friend. Like, when I invited you to Halloween, and she was so mean to you. So if Michelle says something nasty to you, try not to take it personally, OK?"

"OK. I suck it up," Wen said.

Hannah hugged Wen. Then, from her pocket, she got out her iPod and handed Wen one earbud. "Here, you use the right, I'll use the left." Hannah helped Wen fit the earbud snugly into her ear.

Shoulder to shoulder, they rode the rest of the way to school, connected by the wires of the iPod.

By afternoon, the snow had stopped and turned to ice.

"Hurry!" Wen called to Emily, who was skating on the slippery sidewalk.

"What's the big rush?" asked Emily.

"I call Nancy Lin today, try to find family for my friend."

"Cool." Emily picked up her pace.

"This adoption lady is nice, I guess, but she makes me nervous," Wen said.

"Why, Wennie? When Mom and Dad wanted you so bad, that Nancy Lin helped them. She was the one who did all the papers and stuff. And when Mom and Dad were approved, Nancy came over and they were all hugging, Wennie!"

*My mother and father wanted me so bad?* Wen thought. She hadn't considered this before.

She wanted to ask Emily again, just to be sure, but she couldn't bear to get a different answer.

"Hey," Wen called to her mother as she and Emily walked through the front door.

Why couldn't she call her Mom? Emily did it all the time. She could call her father Dad. For some reason, it was only the "Mom" that got stuck like a chicken bone in her throat.

"I call Nancy now?" asked Wen.

"Sure." Her mother showed her Nancy's card.

Wen opened her cell phone and, fingers shaking, she pushed the little numbers. Wen had trouble understanding

English on the phone. She couldn't see the other person's face or read their expressions to help her figure out hard words. As the phone began to ring, Wen's breathing got shallower and shallower.

Wen heard a voice answer. "Hello, this is Nancy."

"Good morning, I am Wen McGuire," began Wen. Immediately she realized she'd gotten the morning part wrong.

"So good to hear from you," Nancy said. "How are you doing, Wen?"

"Fine. My mother said you could find out if my friend on The List. I want to know if her name is here in America. For adopting."

"Ah, the Shared Waiting Child List. Wen, I'm free right now. Why don't you and your mother come by and see The List for yourself?"

An hour later, Nancy greeted Wen and her mother and led them to her small office covered with photographs of beaming American parents and their Chinese children. Mainly, Wen saw babies. Babies in big hats, babies in their mothers' embraces, babies on their fathers' shoulders. Bald babies and babies with thick black hair. All these babies had families.

Wen cringed. *You should be happy for the babies,* she told herself. *They're the lucky ones. They got picked.*

But what about the older kids? What about Shu Ling? What about her?

"Ready?" Nancy beckoned Wen toward her computer. "OK, I've typed in the password. Wen, you must give me your friend's Chinese name, orphanage, and date of birth. Then I can look her up."

Wen hovered by Nancy's desk. *Xie xie. Thank you*, she wanted to say to Nancy. *Thank you for helping me find my friend.*

But she just said, "Shen Shu Ling. Orphanage, Tong Du. I do not know her birthday."

"Her birthday is not a problem. I can find her without the exact date. How old is she?"

"Twelve," said Wen.

Wen glanced over her shoulder at her mother, who nodded reassuringly. She got up to join Wen.

Nancy typed, while Wen and her mother stood behind her. Then she clicked a key to open the screen. It was blank.

"Tell me again. Maybe I entered the information incorrectly."

"Shen Shu Ling. Tong Du." Wen clenched and unclenched her hands.

Nancy Lin's screen stayed blank.

"Oh, Wen," her mother sighed.

"She is not there?" Wen already knew the answer.

Nancy got up from her chair and went to Wen.

"I am so sorry," she said. "Shu Ling is not on The List."

# sixteen

Wen sank onto the folding chair by the wall.

"Not on The List! This means Shu Ling is . . ." Wen choked on the word. "Unadoptable?"

"No, there is reason to hope," said Nancy Lin.

*Hope?* Wen slumped lower. This lady must be joking.

"The Chinese government may have sent your friend Shu Ling straight to a designated agency," Nancy explained. "Those kids aren't on The List. Older kids with severe special needs often get placed with agencies that work extra hard to find them families."

"What is this *des-ig*—" Wen stammered.

"Designated. Picked out," said Nancy. "Shu Ling could be with one of those agencies and maybe that's why she's not on The List."

"Because she has very many special needs?" Wen asked.

*What was so bad about being twelve and having a small clubfoot?*

Wen pulled herself up as tall as she could. "So how we find out if she is there? With a *des-ig-nated* agency?"

"It's not easy." Nancy spoke slowly, as if to be sure Wen understood. "Some designated agencies post their children on a big Web site called Rainbow Kids, which lists lots of adoption agencies. You go to each agency's link and try to find her in their designated children photos. You could start there."

"What if Shu Ling not on Rainbow Kids?" Wen asked. "Sounds like very hard to find."

Then she saw her, standing on the dusty hill, waving at Wen.

"Go over again," said Wen. "Foot by foot."

"I'll go slow," Nancy said. "Step by step."

Wen got out a pencil from her backpack and began to take notes.

"This will be very difficult," said Nancy. "Even if she is with a designated agency, I cannot promise you will find her."

"I find her," Wen vowed.

"Don't spend too much time on Rainbow Kids. Lots of their Web sites need passwords, which you can only get if you've done that agency's adoption paperwork first. Instead, try the online adoption communities." Nancy wrote some Web sites on a piece of paper. "They can help you."

Wen tapped her shoe. "What is this online *com-mun-it-ies?*"

"Communities. Groups of people," said Nancy. "All these people are searching for waiting children too. They have their own online page, where they describe kids they've seen or kids they're looking for."

"Write to strangers?" Wen asked.

"They're not really strangers, because they're all helping each other find kids," Nancy said. "So you go to an online community, say 'Waiting Children,' and you post a profile of Shu Ling, the orphanage she comes from, anything that would help identify her. Somebody might have seen a girl that fits your description, and they would post to tell you where they saw her. They would look out for you."

*Lookout people,* Wen wrote.

"Another thing," Nancy went on. "Be sure to use the advocacy blogs." Nancy wrote down more lines on paper.

"What is this *ad-vo-ca-cy?*" Wen asked.

"It means standing up for something," her mother explained.

"People have blogs where they feature children who need families badly. Once you find Shu Ling," Nancy said, "get her on those blogs standing up for kids, so people will know to go straight to the designated agency and choose her."

*Stand-up people,* Wen scrawled.

As Nancy led them out of her office, Wen avoided the pictures of the little babies again.

"Good luck," Nancy called. "Let me know when you get good news!"

Back home, Wen strode to the computer. "We start?"

"All set." Her mother put on her plastic glasses that made her look like an owl. She sat beside Wen on the other half of the same chair. Wen pushed the On button and tapped her foot on the floor until the screen turned bright blue.

"Nancy say go to the Rainbow Kids first," said Wen.

Her mother guiding her hand on the mouse, Wen opened the Rainbow Kids home page and clicked on the first agency on the list. Children's pictures appeared on the screen. Asian Adoptions Inc. arranged the pictures in neat rows and assigned the kids American names. Wen saw a toddler posing against a brick wall.

> Ben, age 2 years. This adorable boy has a delightful personality. His Chinese name means "hope to face my life bravely." His favorite activity is to be cuddled. Ben was born with cleft palate and bilateral cleft lip, easily repairable by surgery. Although his clefts can impede speech, he has begun to say one- and two-syllable words, including "Mama." This outgoing little guy longs to find his forever family soon.

Wen ached and moved to the next photo.

> Erin. Age 9 years. Severe burns. Erin came into care from a 2-month stay at a hospital, having had a fourth of her skin burnt, due to a fire in her home.

Her parents could not afford the medical
bills. She is cheerful, diligent in her stud-
ies, and enjoys reading fairy tales. She
also takes care of the younger children.
This sweetheart waits for a family to call
her own.

Page after page, Wen saw kids' snapshots arranged like
stamps on sheets at the post office. Only each stamp was a
boy or a girl who wasn't adopted yet.

Wen closed her eyes to shut out the rows of little faces.
Each kid was saying, *Pick me! Pick me!* All these children
seemed to accuse her. *You got picked. You got a family. We're
still waiting.*

Wen forced herself to open her eyes and start again.
How else could she get to Shu Ling?

Beside her, her mother gazed at the screen as if she were
watching a very good movie or thinking about something
that made her smile inside.

"You found me this way?" Wen asked suddenly.

"We did. We fell in love with your little face the minute
we saw you, Wen. We said, 'There she is, our daughter!'"

Her mother paused. "You know, there's an ancient
Chinese legend that says an invisible red thread connects
people who are meant to meet, no matter what. And even
if that thread tangles or stretches, it never breaks."

"This red thread, I have heard of it." Wen stared at the

computer and tried to imagine how her mother and father had seen her picture on the screen and known. Just like that.

"You were ten at the time," Wen's mother went on. "Lots of families choose babies. But we'd already adopted a little baby, Emily. We wanted you."

Wen studied her mother, her eyes glazed, as if she was in a trance or lost in time. A glow of many candles spread across her cheeks.

But suppose her mother and father had skipped her page by accident? Suppose her photo had been in the corner of the screen and her parents had missed it? She almost didn't get picked by them at all.

The awfulness of not being picked by her own parents struck her so hard, she swayed in her chair. Maybe she didn't belong to just anybody. Maybe she belonged to these people—her mother, her father, and Emily, her family.

"Now we will learn about family," Teacher Jun had stated one day at the orphanage, opening his book. With chalk, he scratched on the blackboard:

### *jia ting*—家庭

Family. As if someone had cast a spell on them, the kids sat motionless. Why would Teacher Jun teach them this? The word seemed to taunt Wen.

Next, "Family members." Teacher Jun wrote new characters on the board.

## *mama*—妈妈

*Mama.* An ache like a deep pang had spread through Wen's body. Her arms weak, her hands trembling, she couldn't write the characters naming this person she longed for but would never know and never call by name.

Now, Wen looked over at her mother, whose eyes were soft and inviting. The mama she'd wanted sat right beside her. But when her mother reached out her arms to hug her, all Wen could do was pull away.

Wen turned back to the computer. She pored over each new window, searching for a girl with a thin face, standing with one leg behind the other. Wen gripped the mouse tight. Just one more click, she knew, and that would be the click that led to Shu Ling.

"Wennie." Emily tugged at her elbow. "Come on, read me a book."

"Not now, much work. Later." Wen kept her eyes on the screen.

"You're no fun." Emily pouted.

After dinner, Wen began seeing windows she'd opened earlier. Every kid's picture began to seem the same. After a while, she saw only blurs. None of them was Shu Ling.

The next day, with the heat turned even lower, Wen put on three sweaters. She remembered how Nancy had told her not to spend too much time on Rainbow Kids, to instead go to the online communities, the lookout people. From Nancy's paper, she typed in a Web site address and the words "Waiting Children" appeared on the screen.

Very slowly Wen typed her request.

> I search for my best friend. Has anybody seen her? She is Shen Shu Ling, from Tong Du orphanage, age 12. She has little bit clubfoot and draws pictures, very beautiful. Maybe she is on designated agency, but I cannot find her. If you have seen my best friend, she is like my sister, please tell me where. Very big help.

Then she clicked Post and her words burst online for everybody in the community to read.

Later, Wen found a reply typed under her post. Her heart beat fast. Had someone already found Shu Ling?

> Dear Wen,
>
> Your friend sounds wonderful. We'll keep

looking. We found our first daughter through
this Web site! Don't give up hope.

Wen sighed. No Shu Ling after all.

Where was she?

Back at the orphanage, they had played hide-and-seek,
usually at night because that made the finding harder.

"C'mon, *mei mei!*" Shu Ling would call when the kids
started scrambling in the courtyard. Clutching Shu Ling's
waist, Wen fought the fear that darkness brought.

One night, when Wen was the finder, she pulled Chang
from behind the pile of pipes and grabbed Jin Wei, crouching behind the wall. But where was Shu Ling?

When she finally found Shu Ling that night, wedged
behind the toolshed, Wen clung to her in relief.

But this time, the finding was different, and it wasn't
a game. Wen knew Shu Ling was back at the orphanage,
waiting, all alone.

But was she also on that computer, available for adoption? And if she was, where?

# seventeen

"Guess what Mom just got you at a yard sale!" Emily announced one Sunday in mid-November. "Hurry, Wen!" Emily pulled her down the porch steps. "Look!"

Then Wen saw it: a bicycle.

The only bike Wen had ever seen up close was Cook's, which he pedaled to the orphanage, the front basket heavy with noodle sacks and cabbage. Cook never let the kids try his bike because he said if it broke, the food would rot at the bottom of the hill and they would all have to go hungry.

Wen skimmed her fingers along the bike's handlebars. The frame was the green of spring wheat pushing through warm soil.

"This bike. For me? Whole bike?" Grinning, Wen spread her arms as wide as the bike. "All for me?"

"All yours. I saw it at a yard sale and knew you'd like it," her mother said from behind her.

"Maybe this bike cost much. Maybe an extra?" Wen asked. "Maybe should give back?"

"Don't worry, Wen. It cost eight dollars," her mother reassured her.

"Thank you," Wen said. "Not know how to ride bike, even a little bit. Maybe I fall and break."

"Dad'll teach you," Emily said. "He taught me great."

An hour later, Wen's phone went off, the ringtone set to Hannah.

"What's up?" Hannah asked when Wen picked up.

"Got new bike. From my mother."

"Have you ridden it yet?"

"Too cold maybe. My dad teach me tomorrow after school. Right now he busy, get ready for phone talk job interview for the morning."

"I can teach you today," Hannah said.

Ten minutes later, Hannah rang the doorbell, her own bike propped against the porch.

"There it is. Eight monies!" Wen bounded to her bike, standing on its little leg in the driveway.

"Awesome!" Hannah stroked the green frame.

"OK, you show me?" Wen eyed the beat-up leather bike seat and the handles with little dents where her fingers would fit. "My parents say wear this." Wen showed Hannah a funny plastic hat with slits through the top and a point, like a bird's beak, in the back. "Ugly hat." Wen grimaced.

"Don't worry, I have to wear one too." Hannah poked the helmet dangling from her bike handles.

Hannah helped Wen steer her bike to the sidewalk. "OK. Here's what we'll do. You get on the bike and pedal.

I'll hold on to the seat, running beside you, to keep you up. When I think you're ready, I'll let go."

"I will knock down," said Wen.

"If you fall, it's no big deal. Just get back up. Everybody falls at first."

Wen swung her leg over the seat and settled on the bike.

"Hold on to the handles. That's how you steer. OK, Wen, ready? Just push off, I've got a good grip on the seat."

Wen fit her feet to the pedals and began to pump. The bike lurched forward.

"Great! Keep going, don't stop," Hannah yelled.

*Was Hannah really holding on? Suppose she let go and didn't tell her?*

"You still holding on?" Wen yelled.

"I'll tell you when I let go, I swear."

Wen pedaled faster. Even so, she felt herself weave, the bike teetered, and she clattered to the sidewalk. Her bike landed on top of her.

"OK, Wen?" Hannah hurried toward her, pulled the bike off, and put out her hand. Wen took it and Hannah pulled her to her feet.

Back on the bike, Wen could feel Hannah's grip as she pedaled down the road to the bank parking lot. Her legs stronger, her bike steadier, Wen picked up speed.

"I'm letting go now!" Hannah yelled.

Wen circled the parking lot and fell twice more. Each

time, she got back up. With Hannah jogging beside her, she pushed her legs hard. She stopped wobbling.

"Go, Wen!" Hannah cheered, waving both hands.

Wen sailed around the parking lot.

"You can ride a bike on your own now, Wen! Let's go home and I'll get mine. We can ride together."

Still weaving sometimes, Wen pedaled toward home. She stopped at her porch, where Hannah buckled her helmet and hopped on her bike.

"Let's go! I'll follow you," Hannah yelled.

Wen grasped her handlebars and pumped. Her bike soared. She felt wind against her and pedaled even harder.

"Faster than the wind!" Wen called to Hannah.

"I can't believe you learned in one lesson!" Hannah yelled. "Now we can go everywhere together!"

*Everywhere together.* Wen heard the words and thought of walking with Shu Ling, her *stomp-drag* beside her as they went from the infant room to the courtyard to the hill.

Wen knew she should be back on the computer, tracking down Shu Ling. She'd wasted valuable time today.

*How had she let herself do this?*

Wen slowed her pedaling, lost her balance, and crashed against the curb. Her bike fell on top of her. Hannah stopped and pulled Wen up.

"Are you OK, Wen? What happened to your knee?" Hannah cried.

Wen saw blood dripping down her leg.

"Bleeding not bad. Thanks. Have to go now!" Wen got back on her bike.

"So soon? Are you too hurt to ride more?" asked Hannah.

"I fine. Must go, that's all!" She waved good-bye to Hannah and hurried home to look for Shu Ling.

# eighteen

One afternoon the following week, Wen heard furious snipping in the kitchen. She smelled the glue, suspiciously coming from the same place as the snipping. Then she spied a single neon-blue feather drifting through the air.

Getting off the sofa to investigate, Wen found Emily at the kitchen table, cutting fat pear shapes from brown paper. Biting her lips in concentration, she pasted brightly dyed feathers around the squat bottoms and glued a piece of red yarn at each tip.

"That's the gobbler, Wennie," Emily explained. "Check out all my Thanksgiving turkeys!"

"Good job," said Wen, picking up an orange feather. "We talk about this Thanksgiving in school. Also I see many pictures of cooked turkeys on supermarket flyer. And on computer, so many turkeys, some alive, with fan of feathers. Thanksgiving is big festival in America?"

"Very big deal. You know, we get Thanksgiving and the day after off from school. Didn't you have Thanksgiving in China?" Emily wrinkled her nose, thinking. "No, Wennie, of course not! In China, you didn't! No Plymouth Rock, no big feast, nothing!"

"More door to door this festival?" asked Wen hopefully.

"Nope. But we have a huge dinner. Lots of food, like turkey, stuffing, corn, and pie for dessert. You can have pumpkin pie, Wennie, but I wouldn't recommend it. Mom makes apple, too."

As he loaded the dishwasher, her father dropped a glass, which shattered all over the floor. Muttering, he went to get the broom.

"Watch out, he's in a bad mood," whispered Emily. "I think it's about not finding a job."

"Hunts on computer, no luck." Wen nodded. "This I get."

"Dad, will we be able to get a turkey this Thanksgiving?" asked Emily.

"Pardon me?" Her father seemed far away.

"Is a turkey an extra?" Emily pasted the final feather on one of her fat brown birds.

"No, I think we can afford a turkey this year, Emily," her mother said.

Two days later, Emily came bounding into the kitchen.

"It's Thanksgiving, Wennie!" Emily announced. "Get off the computer."

"Emily, I am hunting for my friend."

"That's all you ever do. What about me? I'm your own sister," Emily wailed.

*She just wants a little attention,* Wen told herself. After all, it was a special day. She shut off the computer.

"OK." Wen faced Emily. "Hi."

"See!" Emily spun around. She was wearing her gray

sweat suit, covered with a stiff white apron. On her head, she'd tied a funny hat that looked like a sailboat.

"Hey, what is this?" Wen knelt beside Emily to admire her. "This festival has costumes too?"

"I was a Pilgrim girl for my class play. You know, Pilgrims? They started America. How do you like my hat?" Emily patted her white hat with flaps on either side.

"Very beautiful Pilgrim girl," said Wen.

Wen smelled the turkey her mother had put in the oven earlier in the morning. The kitchen table was covered with a cloth as white as clouds, and even the silverware seemed to sparkle.

"Grandma Jackson should be here any time now!" said Wen's mother. Then she began to hum.

Wen had never heard her mother hum before.

"Who you say this lady is?" Wen moved closer to the oven to hear her mother's humming better.

"You've seen her in the photo album, Wen. She's my mother. More of your family. She can't wait to meet her new granddaughter." She paused. "That must be the car now!"

Wen heard her father's voice booming and the front door open. Behind her father, she saw a tall woman with wiry gray hair and eyes as blue as her mother's.

"Mother!" Wen's mother nearly flew over to Grandma Jackson. She hugged her for a long time.

Then, her arm still around Grandma Jackson, her mother drew Wen toward her.

"Mother, meet your new granddaughter."

"Welcome to our family, Wen." Wen's grandmother's arms wrapped around her tight, and Wen smelled the fragrance of violets.

"Grandma!" Emily hurled herself at Grandma Jackson.

"Oh, my girls." She embraced Wen and Emily at the same time. "Such beautiful sisters!"

Wen pulled away. She didn't mean to. But when anybody said *sisters*, she automatically thought of Shu Ling, her real sister.

When Wen stepped back, Emily fled from the kitchen, sniffing as though she might cry.

"What's wrong with Em?" Grandma Jackson asked.

"Nothing time won't fix, Mother," said Wen's mother.

After they'd eaten cheese and crackers in the living room for ages, Wen followed the rest of the family to the kitchen. Her mother brought out the sizzling turkey.

"Kind of smallish this year," said Emily.

Oh, if Emily could see the noodles and dumplings the kids ate every day at the orphanage. Wen wished Shu Ling could eat some of this turkey.

"We should say what we're grateful for," said her mother.

"I'm grateful I've had some phone interviews," said her father.

*But not a job*, Wen thought.

"I'm grateful our family is all here, all healthy," her mother said.

Wen tensed. If she'd asked earlier, before her father got laid off, Shu Ling would be at this table too.

"Pass," said Emily.

"Emily McGuire, you cannot pass," her father scolded. "Surely you can think of something to be grateful for."

Emily sighed. "Grateful for Wennie, even if she doesn't think I'm her sister."

Gazing down at Emily's tiny little face, Wen half wanted to gather her into her lap and snuggle with her. Then she caught herself. Emily might be her sister now, but Shu Ling was her first, true sister, since a long time ago.

Grandma Jackson said she was grateful for everything good in her life, especially her beautiful granddaughters.

Everybody turned toward Wen.

"I am grateful I am here," Wen said.

After the meal, Wen and Emily cleaned up. Wen scrubbed the counters especially hard and mopped the kitchen floor with bleach.

Then Wen went outside and sat on the porch steps, staring at the bare tree branches against the gray sky. She should be thankful on this Big Turkey festival. But instead, she kept wishing Shu Ling had a family too. Then she could be really grateful.

When she finally went back inside, she caught Grandma Jackson, wearing tiny little wire glasses, perched at the computer.

"What you doing, Grandma?"

"Your mother says you've been online, trying very hard to find your friend Shu Ling," Grandma Jackson said. "So I thought I'd take a little look-see, help you out some."

"Thanks, Grandma," said Wen. "This helps much."

Her grandmother folded Wen into her arms and Wen did not pull back. It seemed OK to hug this nice lady who was her grandma. Was hugging her mother's mother almost as good as hugging her own mother?

Right before bed, after all the food was put away and Grandma Jackson had gone home, Wen clicked on the online communities page again. This time there was a message for her.

> Dear Wen,
>
> I think I have found your friend. Go to the Worldwide Adoptions waiting child page and see. Good luck!

Frantic, Wen typed in the Worldwide Adoptions address and went to the page of waiting children. She went to a description and clicked.

Wen gasped. Then she blinked and looked again.

Shu Ling!

# nineteen

Wen gazed at Shu Ling's high-cheeked face, her braid pulled back with a piece of twine. Wen would know that profile anywhere.

"Hey!" Wen shouted. "Come quick! I found Shu Ling!"

Wen's mother tore down from the attic, followed by Emily, toothpaste dribbling from her chin. Wen's father came next, computer glasses in his hand.

"I found her!" Wen shrieked, jumping up and down.

"What great news!" her mother said.

While her mother, father, and Emily crowded around the computer, Wen printed out the faded photograph. Wen figured the picture was about two years out of date. Shu Ling seemed especially thin as she teetered awkwardly on her turned-in leg, a forlorn smile across her sallow cheeks.

Susie. Age 13. Clubfoot. Available for
just under seven weeks, since by Chinese
policy, Susie must be adopted before she

turns 14, when she ages out and can no
longer be placed with a family.

"Name is not Susie. And what is this 'age out'?" Wen
demanded.

"Says here Shu Ling's thirteen. The day she turns fourteen, she's too old to be adopted," her mother explained.

"How come?" Wen asked. "Who says this?"

"It's a rule made by the Chinese government," her mother
answered. "Fourteen is too old. That's the Chinese rule."

"But Shu Ling not thirteen," said Wen. "She is twelve."

"Are you sure, honey?" her mother asked.

"Everybody know this," Wen stated. "Ever since I came
to orphanage. Shu Ling one year older than me. All the
aunties know. Shu Ling turned twelve last year."

"When is Shu Ling's birthday?" Wen's father asked.

"Don't know exact day. Aunties and kids don't pay much
attention to date in file. Everybody just move up one year
on Lunar New Year."

"Well, the official date in her file is the one the government uses," Wen's mother said. "We know your birthday is
in April because the orphanage doctor measured your head
and estimated your age. That's what happens for all the kids.
A doctor decides an official date and puts it in the file."

"Shu Ling is not thirteen," Wen protested. "I get the real
date and get this fixed right away."

Otherwise Shu Ling would never have time to get picked by a family. Not in less than seven weeks.

"I call this Worldwide place," Wen went on. "Tell them Shu Ling is twelve."

"They're closed right now. It's Thanksgiving, sweetie," her mother said.

"I call Monday morning as soon as they open."

"You'll be at school, Wen. You can call as soon as you get home."

"But I call when they open. Fix Shu Ling's birthday."

"School first, call later," said her mother.

On Monday morning, Wen stayed in bed past breakfast.

She clutched her belly when her mother tried to wake her up. "I not good."

Her mother sat by her bed. "You seemed fine yesterday."

"It just come. It is possible I throw up. At school this happen, very bad. People see." Wen huddled under her covers, eyeing her phone by her pillow. "I stay home today."

Wen's mother crossed her arms, thinking.

"Must stay home," Wen said.

"OK. But your stomach has to feel better tomorrow."

"Oh, much better tomorrow," Wen said.

Her mother started to close the door. "If they don't pick up at nine o'clock, try again at nine fifteen, Wen. Sometimes people don't answer their phones right away on Mondays."

Wen caught her mother's eye. Wen knew she knew.

*Thank you*, she wanted to say to her mother. But she couldn't.

"I sleep now. Very sick." Wen turned over and pretended to doze off.

She called at 9:01.

"Good morning, this is Worldwide Adoptions, Jenny Peters speaking."

"I see on your Web site, Susie, age thirteen," Wen said.

"I'm sorry," said Jenny Peters. "Can I put you on hold?"

Wen heard the phone switch to boring music. Now her stomach really did hurt. She had so much to tell this lady, she thought she might burst. Suppose she didn't have enough English for all she needed to say? Suppose she talked about Shu Ling and started to cry?

"OK, here I am." Jenny Peters sounded so cheerful she almost chirped. "You were calling about Susie? Let's see, her real name is Shen Shu Ling. We use the American name for privacy."

"I know this girl," Wen heard herself stammer. She stared at Shu Ling's portrait on the bulletin board, which seemed to ground her. "I am Wen. Shu Ling's best friend."

"You actually *know* Susie?" said Jenny Peters. Wen could almost see her raising her eyebrows.

"Shu Ling. She was my best friend back at the orphanage.

Long time. I know her much." Wen heard herself speaking good English.

"But your Web site say she is thirteen," Wen continued. "I know her right age. Shu Ling is twelve. Aunties know this, kids know this."

"Hold on. Let me get her file."

Again Wen heard the annoying music.

"Back again. Yes, according to our records, the Tong Du orphanage file states that Shen Shu Ling was born on January 12, thirteen years ago. So that's her official birthday."

Shu Ling couldn't be thirteen! These Worldwide people were wrong.

"We call," Wen proposed. "Tell them file not right."

"The files are official, Wen. We never find mistakes in the birth dates," Jenny said.

"If this true, this mean Shu Ling not have much time," Wen protested.

"We've had her on our Web site a while, way beyond the usual deadline, and so far, no family has expressed interest. When she turns fourteen, she'll age out."

"My mother explain this age out. Happens to old girls, not like Shu Ling. Shu Ling a younger girl."

"I'm so sorry. On January 12, she'll be fourteen and we'll have to send her file back to China. So your friend has to be picked *before* her actual birthday. Otherwise it's too late."

"OK, then, I help you work fast." Wen spoke loudly into

her phone. "You not know Shu Ling like I do. Under very old photo, not say many words."

"We usually just give the identifying information, until a family indicates interest."

"How anybody pick Shu Ling if they don't know her?" said Wen. "I tell you more."

"You want to rewrite her whole description? We rarely do this. It seems fine the way it is." Jenny Peters's cheerful voice turned terse. "Maybe you should talk to our agency writer. He'll be in tomorrow."

"Better to tell you now," Wen said. "I tell, you listen. Then you put what I say under her picture. So somebody picks her better. This girl, she is my friend, like sister." Wen paused. "She needs family fast. Today your Web site say little over six weeks."

"A day over six weeks," Jenny Peters murmured. "All right. It goes against our policy, but since you do know her so well . . ." Jenny said. "I'm at my computer. Go ahead."

"Shu Ling," Wen began. "She is twelve." Wen waited for Jenny to correct her, but she kept on typing, so maybe even Jenny thought the age might be wrong. "She has a clubfoot, little bit. Walks fine, nothing to worry about. She helps the aunties with the babies. She can scrub the tiles and also she cook noodles, mix baby drink. Also she draws pictures, so beautiful. She waits for a family for a long time. Pick her and you will be happy ever after."

"Just a minute, I think I've got it all."

"Also, Shu Ling good artist. We post a portrait she did, so people know she has talent, like a celebrity?"

"I'll scan in the picture as soon as you send it. This is a little unusual, Wen, but we'll do our best. It'll be up by Friday."

"Thanks." Wen hesitated. "Wednesday would also be good day."

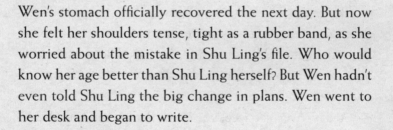

Wen's stomach officially recovered the next day. But now she felt her shoulders tense, tight as a rubber band, as she worried about the mistake in Shu Ling's file. Who would know her age better than Shu Ling herself? But Wen hadn't even told Shu Ling the big change in plans. Wen went to her desk and began to write.

> Dear Shu Ling,
>
> I've wanted to tell you this but I've been waiting until I had some good news for you. A little while ago, my father lost his job, and now my parents don't have the money to adopt you. I am so sorry about this, Shu Ling. I waited until I knew they would say yes but my father got fired before I could even ask. I wish so much I had asked sooner! I also haven't wanted to tell you because I have let you down.

But now my mother is helping me find you a family of your own, another way. You'll still have a family and we can still visit each other here in America. I'm sorry it's not possible about my family. But we can see each other all the time. We have vacations in America and we can spend them together. Maybe whole summers.

For me to find you this family, I have to know something:

Please tell me, you are twelve years old, right? Let me know as soon as you can.

Love,

Wen

From her wallet, she counted all the allowance money she'd saved until her parents declared allowances were an extra. Wen put her letter and wallet with twelve dollars and five cents in her parka pocket and walked to the post office.

"Like to mail this to China as fast as possible," Wen said to the woman behind the desk, who placed her letter on a scale.

"To China, express delivery, forty-seven dollars and ninety-five cents," she said.

Wen frowned. "How about less fast?" she asked.

"That'll be ninety-eight cents," said the woman.

Wen counted out her change and the woman stamped

her letter. "Should get there next week or the week after at the latest."

Next week and then maybe two weeks for Shu Ling to write back and in the meantime, the false date was still on the Web site, the aging out still happening.

le

At dinner, Wen swirled her fork in the pasta, not eating. "Cannot believe Shu Ling's age is wrong."

Wen's father shook his head. "If it's in her file, Wen, there's nothing else we can do."

"Auntie Lan Lan know," said Wen. "Maybe there are two dates in file. Maybe people using wrong date, should be using the twelve-year-old date."

"How would Auntie Lan Lan know?" her mother asked.

"Auntie Lan Lan good spy. She know everything that goes on. Besides, she in charge of files. I call her, just to be sure. Otherwise, age out will happen."

Wen's mother glanced at her watch. "It's seven in the morning at the orphanage. Do you want to call now?"

Wen knew calling the orphanage would be really expensive. "You are sure? Very large extra," Wen said.

"Sometimes there are extras you can't cut out, Wen," said her mother.

*Just hug her,* Wen told herself, flooded with gratitude. But she couldn't.

Wen's mother copied the orphanage phone number for Wen and handed her the phone.

"*Ni hao.*" Wen heard a voice she'd know anywhere.

"Auntie Lan Lan, it's me, Wen."

"Ah, Wen! You called us!" Auntie Lan Lan shouted, as if her voice needed to cross the ocean.

"Auntie Lan Lan, do you know Shu Ling's birth date? The exact date? There's been a big mistake. The people over here think she's thirteen."

"Thirteen." Wen heard Auntie Lan Lan sigh. "Almost too old for adoption."

"Right," said Wen. "So can you check her file, to be sure? Maybe there is a scratch-out. Maybe somebody read it wrong."

"Director Feng is on a trip. I'll go to the files in his office and pick up the phone there. You hold on, OK?"

In the background, Wen could hear the babies. She'd forgotten how loudly the babies cried, how the air seemed to pulse with their wailing.

Auntie Lan Lan's voice came back on the phone. "I have it."

"Read me her birth date, Auntie Lan Lan."

"It says Shen Shu Ling was born thirteen years ago. So she turns fourteen this January 12."

"Go over it again. Is there another date somewhere on the page?"

"No, Wen. That's it. I remember now how, in the beginning, when Shu Ling came here, there were so many babies all left at the same time. The aunties tried, Wen, but some of them got the birth dates mixed up. So early on, especially because Shu Ling was so malnourished, we must have thought she was a year younger and kept using that age. But the file is right, it gives the official date."

"This," Wen gasped, "this cannot be possible."

"She is thirteen now. Wen, I am sorry," whispered Auntie Lan Lan.

"It's OK, Auntie Lan Lan. It's not your fault," Wen said. "I must go now. Thank you for answering my question."

Suddenly, there was so little time left.

"Of course, Wen. Maybe you will find a family for Shu Ling even so," Wen heard Auntie Lan Lan say.

"Maybe. Bye, Auntie Lan Lan." Wen hung up quickly, so Auntie Lan Lan wouldn't hear her crying in America.

# twenty

Out her window the next morning, Wen saw the dark skies split open and rain pound down.

"Richard," her mother called from the sink. "We've got a leak!"

Wen and Emily tore into the kitchen, where water was collecting on the ceiling and dripping onto the stove. Just as her mother put a big pot under the leak, two other drips started, near the middle of the ceiling. Her mother grabbed two more pots.

"I thought we got the roof fixed last year," her father fumed.

*Extra*, thought Wen. *Fixed roof an extra.*

They took turns dumping out the water from the pots. Soon the ceiling paint began to peel, turning the drippings a milky white.

"There goes the ceiling," her mother said with a sigh, as she massaged her forehead.

*Ceiling an extra*, Wen noted.

The streaming water beat against the metal pots.

"This noise is killing me," her mother complained.

Wen stuffed towels into the containers and the dripping sounds softened.

"Oh, thank you, Wen," her mother said.

"This we do in the orphanage," Wen said.

Later, the sun came out. The dripping stopped, and Wen's mother put the pots away. Nobody mentioned the peeling ceiling.

Emily put on polka-dot rain boots and splashed in puddles in the backyard.

"Christine, the basement, come quick!" her father called.

Wen and her mother sized up the basement, where her father stood in a foot of murky black water.

"The ground's so wet, water must be seeping through the foundation," her mother said. "We've known the foundation's had cracks for a while now."

"Can't deal with the whole foundation now, that's for sure." Her father grabbed a bucket and began to bail water into the basement sink.

*Foundation of house an extra,* Wen thought.

What was next to go?

⌒⌒

After Wen, Emily, and her mother helped her father bail out the basement, Wen got out paper and a ruler. She made rows and columns for the months of December and January. Then, with purple marker, she colored a huge star in the box of January 11, the day before Shu Ling's fourteenth birthday. That was the last day a family could pick Shu Ling. She'd make a black X on each day that passed without success. The blank boxes were the days full of possibility, days when Shu Ling might be chosen. Across the top, with a thick red marker, Wen wrote the word

## COUNTDOWN!

It was December the first. According to Wen's calendar, just under six weeks now remained until Shu Ling's final day.

On Friday, Wen opened the Worldwide Adoptions Web site to see the new description Jenny Peters had assured her would be ready. But the same old, weary one reappeared.

Wen called Jenny. "It's Friday. Day of the new Web site. It comes today?"

"Wen, I'm so sorry. Things got held up on our end," said Jenny. "The Web site person is telling me Sunday, now."

Wasted days! Wen's panic rose. "Sunday the latest, please! Days fly fast." She glanced at the calendar, its empty boxes almost screaming, "Five weeks and four days left."

When Wen clicked onto the Worldwide Adoptions Web site on Sunday, Shu Ling's listing was updated at last.

**This 13-Year-Old Girl
Needs a Family Now!**

**Pick This Treasure Before She Ages Out
in a Little Over 5 Weeks!**

Susie is thirteen and will age out January
12. She has a clubfoot, correctible by
surgery. She is a delightful girl who helps
the aunties feed the babies and gives
extra love to the neediest children. She
cooks very tasty noodles. She scrubs tiles
until they shine, weeds well, and does all
chores with the greatest energy. Susie
has a cheerful disposition and a sunny
smile. This girl is an artist, gifted with
special talent. She has waited for a forever family for a long time. Contact Jenny
Peters for additional information about
how you can make Susie your daughter.

A new photograph, the one Shu Ling had sent Wen,
showed Shu Ling standing on top of the hill. She wore the
red good-luck tunic Wen had sent her and her flared jeans
so her bad leg wouldn't show. Even though Shu Ling's face
looked gaunt and pinched, she smiled bravely, as if to say,
*Pick me, great daughter!* Underneath her picture was the portrait of Wen and Shu Ling that Wen's father had helped
scan, the lines so gentle, the shading so fine, it showed Shu
Ling's talent far better than words.

Now a family was bound to pick Shu Ling. Now some family would say, just like Wen's own family did, *There's our daughter. We choose her.*

Because she had practically memorized Nancy's step-by-step list, Wen could almost hear Nancy's voice, brimming with hopefulness. *Once you find her,* she had said, *get her on the advocacy blogs of the stand-up people.* They would post Shu Ling's picture and direct people to Worldwide Adoptions, to adopt her.

Wen attached her own picture of Shu Ling, the description, and the portrait to e-mails she sent to the advocacy blog writers. By the next day, all had responded.

"Great girl. I'll feature her," wrote Sandy from "Children Who Wait." "You're a wonderful friend to be doing this."

"Thanks for sending this. I'll post it right away," replied a blog person named Linda, who had a site called "Forever Families."

"I'm on it," said Tom, from his "Take Me Home" blog.

"We'll find her a family as soon as we can," Donna wrote from "Needed: One Family." When Wen opened the blogs again, she saw Shu Ling on each one, her write-up and portrait just below her picture, with a link to the Worldwide Adoptions Web site so people would find her right away.

Five weeks and one day left.

Every day Shu Ling wasn't picked, Wen drew a black X through a square on her countdown calendar. As a week passed with nothing happening, the blog people got as anxious as she was.

Dear Wen,

I see a family hasn't picked your friend yet. Don't give up. We're calling her our Child of the Week. Hopefully this will bring her a lot of attention.

Sandy

Hi Wen,

No news from our Shu Ling advocacy. We've sent out a special blog alert to all our readers. Try not to worry. Somebody's bound to pick her soon.

Keep the faith,

Tom

Another storm came, the rain beating against the roof. Wen listened for leaks and wondered how the foundation was holding up. When she clicked on Shu Ling's photo, as she did several times a day, Shu Ling remained familyless. Exactly four weeks were left.

What was going wrong? Wen dialed Jenny Peters to see if she knew.

"Wen, I'm glad you called," Jenny said. "The phone is ringing off the hook. We're getting such a response to the new description of Shu Ling. All of a sudden, people want to know about her. In the past week alone, her page got fifty-four hits."

"Hits? What is this hits?" Wen asked.

"Clicks. People who read the words you wrote about her. Eighteen hits just yesterday, Wen. I've never seen anything like it. Nobody in the office has either. You've done a remarkable job. The blog readers are coming our way too. You must have covered every blog out there, Wen! Somebody's bound to pick her."

"But have only four more weeks. All those hits and nobody say yes?" Wen asked.

"Not yet, but lots of activity, Wen. I've also had six or seven families call me directly, to ask more about her. I'll let you know as soon as I hear anything."

*Hits*, Wen thought as she clicked her phone shut. When would one of those hits lead to a family who picked Shu Ling?

A couple of days later, a letter arrived from Shu Ling. Wen tore open the envelope.

Dear Mei Mei,

I just got your letter and then yesterday, Auntie Lan Lan told me you had called. Yes, I am thirteen years old after all. She and I went over the file together. I wanted to be sure. And all those years we thought I was just a year older than you!

I am so sad I cannot be in your family. But it is OK, Wen. We'll visit each other in America and still see each other. I like the idea of spending summers with each other. We'll still find ways to be together. That's what matters.

Auntie Lan Lan told me about the age-out rule. Me being thirteen is bad for getting me a family, right? Just do your best, mei mei. I know you will.

Love,

Shu Ling

P.S. If you can't find me a family, don't feel bad. I could always be an auntie.

"I could always be an auntie," Shu Ling had said one

day last spring, just after Wen got picked for adoption. They were collecting smooth pebbles near the orphanage walkway.

"On your feet all day?" Wen had asked. "Don't you see how tired the aunties get standing so long, especially when they're older?"

Wen looked discreetly at Shu Ling's turned-in leg. How many hours a day could Shu Ling work, with that twisted leg?

"Besides," Wen continued, "you always get so attached to all the babies, Shu Ling, and when the sick ones die, you get sad for such a long time. If you were an auntie your whole life, you'd get your heart broken, over and over."

"But if I am not an auntie, then what?" Shu Ling had sighed, sifting through some pebbles.

"Well, think of the other older girls who left. Li Wei and Chen went to work at the chemical plant up north," Wen said.

"I could do that, *mei mei*," said Shu Ling.

Wen thought, then shook her head. "The fumes made those girls sick and they had to quit."

Shu Ling put down a stone, selected another, then tossed it away too. "Jin Jing worked as a coal mining receptionist."

*Until the coal dust blackened her lungs*, Wen thought to herself.

"Mei Lin became a manicurist in the city. Somebody would hire me, Wen," Shu Ling said.

Wen patted Shu Ling's arm but said nothing. She had heard too much from Director Feng. People like him wouldn't hire Shu Ling, not with a disability like her leg.

"Shu Ling, what you really need is a family. Remember our agreement? Whoever got picked first would find a family for the other. It's up to me now. I give you my word, Shu Ling! I'll find you a family as soon as I get to America," Wen had vowed.

Now Wen counted on her fingers. Three weeks and five days left. And then, if Shu Ling was still without a family, Wen would have broken that promise forever.

# twenty-one

"Wen," Hannah whispered in class on Friday afternoon as they got out boards and clay to work on their anatomy project. "Can you come to my house tomorrow? I just got a cool new jewelry kit."

"Make jewelry?" Wen widened her eyes.

"Even earrings!"

Should she go to Hannah's? What about following Shu Ling's photo online? There wasn't much time left to find Shu Ling a family. Maybe there were some advocacy blogs she'd missed.

Still, Hannah had invited her to come. And Wen had always longed to make jewelry.

"I come. Short while," Wen said.

"Hannah and Wen, are you working over there?" asked Ms. Beckwith.

"We're really working, Ms. Beckwith." Hannah nudged Wen with her elbow. "We just shaped the kidney, like a kidney bean, right, Wen?"

"Yes," Wen chimed in. "And made some veins, very thin."

"So you'll come, right?" Hannah whispered.

"Be there." Wen molded a long esophagus and, together, they placed it on the board.

"This poor person could use some jewelry." Hannah giggled. "Especially a necklace."

Wen clapped her hand over her mouth, so Ms. Beckwith wouldn't hear her laughter.

Wen couldn't remember the last time she'd laughed like that. Her laughter felt like little bubbles, rising and fizzing inside her.

The next day, Wen walked over to Hannah's with some red velvet cupcakes Emily had left over from a class party.

"Oh, yum, cupcakes!" Hannah said. She led Wen to her bedroom, which had a bed covered with veils.

"You sleep like princess!" Wen exclaimed.

"Yeah. A princess with two houses." Hannah went to the kitchen and came back with napkins for the cupcakes. "Here's the kit. See, we have lots and lots of beads, every color."

"These are jewelry you have made? So beautiful!" Wen marveled at the sparkly necklaces hanging from a small tree made of white iron.

"I do jewelry all the time."

The girls sat on Hannah's bed and dumped out the little boxes of beads between them.

"Oh, love the diamond ones." Wen picked up a sparkly bead that glimmered in the sunlight.

"These black ones are nice too." Hannah put a shiny

black droplet in Wen's palm. "So you make up your design, like which colors you're going to use, and then you cut some wire with these scissors," said Hannah.

"Where you get this kit?" Wen scooped up as many sparkly blue and purple diamonds as she could find.

"My dad. I guess he feels bad because he doesn't see me that much." Hannah bit into a cupcake and lowered her voice. "Last year, you know what I made him?"

Wen glanced at Hannah, her curly head bent low, her long fingers sliding bead after bead onto the silver wire in her lap.

"I made him a tie clip out of shiny black beads. I thought it would look cool in his business meetings and all. Then maybe he'd see how much I wished he'd come back, you know?"

Wen nodded. "He liked the tie clip?"

"He said he did. But after he left, Wen, I found it in its box, under the bed. He didn't even take it."

"No!" Wen protested. "This you made for your father, special. He was wrong to do this."

"So too bad for him. That was his last chance." Hannah peered over at Wen, who was stringing a long necklace of diamond beads. "Is that for your friend in China?"

Wen nodded. "Found her on Web site but no family pick her yet. Just three and a half weeks left."

"That stinks," Hannah said. "Hey, show me the Web site."

Hannah opened her laptop and Wen went to the

Worldwide Adoptions Web site and clicked on Shu Ling's page.

"Wow!" Hannah held the laptop closer. "She drew this amazing picture?"

"Very good artist," said Wen.

"And all the stuff you wrote about her, Wen!" Hannah exclaimed.

"You like it?" Wen asked.

"Yes! Shu Ling is on the *Internet*, Wen! The Internet goes all over the whole world, you know that, right? Everywhere. People with certain phones could even find her on their touch screens! Some family somewhere is bound to pick Shu Ling this way. How can they not, with such an awesome profile of her?"

Wen beamed. "You think so?"

"Wen. It'll happen any day now," Hannah said.

They finished their necklaces. Hannah's was a choker, made of black beads interspersed with round pearls.

"Let's wear our necklaces and I'll take a photo with my cell phone," Hannah suggested.

She positioned her head against Wen's and extended the phone to arm's length. Then Hannah snapped the shutter and there on the screen, Wen saw the two of them, grinning broadly, their necklaces glowing.

"Mom, come see the picture we took," Hannah said as she led Wen into the kitchen. She showed her mother her phone.

"Great picture!" Hannah's mother said. "You two look like the best of friends."

*The best of friends.* Wen recoiled, then caught herself.

"Wen, do stay for dinner. We're having pasta and home-made pesto. We'd love to have you, right, Hannah?"

"Please stay, Wen," Hannah begged.

Wen kept her eyes on the phone screen, where she and Hannah tilted their heads together, as if they'd been friends forever.

"Thank you, this is not possible," said Wen. "I have to go now."

"What's up, Wen? You just got here!" Hannah said.

"Must get home, very late. Hannah, thanks for jewelry. Had such a nice time."

She didn't wait for Hannah to try to convince her to stay. As she hurried home she heard Hannah's mother saying *best of friends* over and over.

But Shu Ling was her best friend, her longest friend, with nobody else to count on. Wen couldn't ever forget that.

# twenty-two

As the holidays neared, Wen noticed that the blogs made a big deal about adopting children. They featured extra kids, they made the titles bigger. Holidays were for families and families needed kids, was how the blogs put it.

On Sandy's blog, in letters twinkling like little lights around Shu Ling's thin face, Wen read, "A Little Over Three Weeks Left! Bring This Girl into Your Family Now!"

Tom, who wrote on his "Take Me Home" blog every day, had created a special link to Shu Ling, where, beneath the portrait of Wen and Shu Ling, red words said "Her friend loves her. You will too!"

Still, Shu Ling's photo stayed on the Worldwide Web site, unchosen. Wen called Jenny to see what she thought.

"We're still getting plenty of hits, Wen," Jenny Peters reported. "Remember it slows down a little during the holidays."

"Thought it went faster," Wen said.

"A lot can happen in three weeks and a day," Jenny Peters said.

Later, as Wen stared at the blank squares left on her

calendar, she tried to cheer herself with Jenny Peters's words. A lot could happen in twenty-two days. A family could pick Shu Ling.

Or she could lose her best friend for good.

ℓℓ

That afternoon, Wen's mother took Wen and Emily Christmas shopping.

"Not spend much monies," Wen reminded Emily. "Dad said mall special just treat because of festival."

At the mall-palace, Wen used her savings to buy her father a coffee mug. He always used the same cracked cup when he hunted for jobs. While her mother waited on the bench outside the store, she and Emily bought her citrus oil in a lemon-shaped bottle.

"She always smell good," Wen said.

"Mom, you mean?" Emily swung the plastic shopping bag.

"Yeah, her," Wen said.

When Emily was with her mother, Wen bought Emily a soft white bear with a pink bow at its neck. She could imagine Emily settling her new bear on her pillow beside all her other stuffed animals.

Downstairs, Wen saw a long line of kids waiting to sit on the lap of a man dressed like Santa Claus.

"Wennie, did you have Santa at the orphanage?" Emily asked.

"Yes. Auntie Mu Hong brought back big poster of Santa from the city and taped it to the wall. Forgot to take down, so Santa, he stayed up until July."

"In America, kids think he brings toys."

"In orphanage, kids know this not true," Wen said.

On Wednesday, Wen's father came home wearing a red polo shirt with big orange letters, "RE," on the right pocket.

"What's up with the shirt, Daddy?" Emily asked.

"I'm working as a salesperson at Regal Electronics until I find a computer job," said her father. "They had an unexpected opening."

"Very nice shirt," Wen said politely.

"Thanks. Now help me get our tree into the house." Her father motioned toward a pine tree tied to his car roof.

Wen and Emily grabbed the top of the tree while their father held the trunk, and together they heaved it into the living room. Wen's mother brought out big boxes. Wen and Emily looped little colored lights from branch to branch. Then everybody hung the decorations—shiny balls, lacy snowflakes, and glittery stars. When they'd finished, Wen lay on the carpet and wedged her head so close under the tree boughs that the lowest needles tickled her nose. She inhaled the fresh, clean scent of pine.

At the orphanage, Christmas had mostly been just like

any other day, except sometimes Cook splashed extra vin-egar on their dumplings or served sweet buns. There had been no tree inside.

"It's Wennie's first Christmas!" Emily snuggled beside Wen and gazed up at the tree too.

"Like tree best," said Wen.

"Glad it's not an extra," Emily whispered.

"And Grandma Jackson's coming again." From under the tree, Wen could hear the lilt in her mother's voice.

"Grandma brings good presents," Emily commented. "What do you want for Christmas, Wen?"

"I am without clue," said Wen.

"You mean *clueless*," Emily corrected her.

"Have everything," Wen answered.

But it wasn't true. She had everything but the thing that mattered most: a family for Shu Ling.

$$\mathcal{el}$$

"Guess what? My dad's coming home for Christmas dinner!" Hannah told Wen at the bus stop the next morning.

On the way to school, Wen noticed Hannah swaying in her seat, her gaze faraway, as if she was daydreaming. Wen decided she was probably thinking about how she and her dad would hug when he came inside for the big banquet.

That was what she and Shu Ling would do, if Shu Ling were here, visiting for Christmas, along with her whole new family. They'd hug. Then Wen would show her the tree and they'd lie under it together. Shu Ling would love the tree. And then she'd say, *Oh*, mei mei, *I can't believe I'm here, and for Christmas, too!*

$$\infty$$

"Mail, Wennie," Emily called the day before Christmas. Wen ripped open the envelope and read the Chinese characters, as delicate as the tracks of tiny birds.

Dear Mei Mei,

We just had a very large snowstorm. The orphanage ran out of coal and we didn't have heat for days. My bad leg got very big. It was white and puffy and hurt like somebody was sticking little pins in it. Dr. Han came. He was mad and he said, "Why didn't anybody soak this leg for you?" Then Dr. Han soaked my leg himself and wrapped it in towels. He told Auntie Bi Yu she must always watch my leg for frostbite, that if nobody kept my leg warm, next time, he might have to cut it off.

Maybe I will see you by the time the snow melts, in the spring! Oh please, mei mei, find me a family fast as you can.

Love from your Shu Ling

Wen put down the letter. Not Shu Ling's leg!

Last winter the furnace had broken down and the orphanage was so cold, Shu Ling's twisted leg swelled and turned waxy and pale. In a week, her skin, now the color of reddish earth, became hard and numb. From the kitchen, Wen carried a heavy pail of warm water to Shu Ling's bed, soaking her leg every half hour. When the electricity had gone off days later, Wen couldn't heat the water on the stove anymore, so she had wrapped herself around Shu Ling's leg, keeping it warm with her own body heat.

Finally Dr. Han came. He said if Shu Ling's leg got too badly frostbitten, blood-filled blisters would appear and then the blood would stop flowing to her leg altogether. Her deadened and shrunken skin would turn black. He'd have to amputate.

Then Wen heard him say something else to Auntie Bi Yu. "*Huai si,*" he whispered. *Gangrene.* If Shu Ling's bad leg stayed too cold for too long, tissue death, caused by lack of blood, would set in. Her joints and nerves and tendons would decay and her muscles and bones would rot. She would no longer be able to move. Then her body temperature would fall so low, Shu Ling's lungs would begin to shut down. Then her brain would stop working right and she would become very confused. Finally, her heart failing, Shu Ling would lose consciousness. And then she would die.

Now Wen clutched Shu Ling's letter so tightly, she almost crushed the paper.

*Huai si!* Not *huai si!*

Wen zipped up her parka and fled to the backyard hill, hurling her body into the cold wind. Even over the icy blasts, she could hear the words *Huai si! Huai si!* still haunting her.

Wen reached the top of the hill, her hair whipping against her face. If she ran up and down the hill hard enough, the sound of her heart pounding would block out the *huai si* words and, finally, buffeted by the wind, she'd go completely numb.

Bracing herself, Wen tore down the slope, then hurling her body against the strong currents, she pushed her way back up again. After charging up and down the hill more times than she could count, she couldn't fight the wind any longer. Shivering and exhausted, she went inside, Shu Ling's letter wadded in her reddened hands.

"What's wrong, sweetie?" Wen's mother asked later that night as the family gathered around the fire, drinking cocoa. "It's Christmas Eve and you're very quiet."

"Got bad news from Shu Ling," Wen said. "Her leg got too cold. The club one. Means might have to get leg cut off." Wen couldn't tell about the rest. It was too awful to talk about.

"Oh, no!" Wen's father put his arm around Wen.

"Somebody has to soak it, like I did, or very bad things happen!" Wen said.

"Wen, I'm sure somebody will take care of Shu Ling's leg," said her mother. "The aunties will be on top of it."

"Not enough aunties at the orphanage," Wen said. "Might not remember."

When the neon numbers on her clock said two in the morning, Wen was still awake. She got up, turned on her desk light, and wrote.

> Dear Shu Ling,
>
> I am very worried about you! Please be very careful of your leg.
> Remember to ask Auntie Bi Yu to soak your leg the minute it gets cold. You should put it in a bucket of lukewarm water every half hour and then you should put plenty of towels over it, until the next soak. Your leg can't get too cold or some very bad things might happen.
> I miss you every day.
>
> Love from your mei mei

On Christmas Day, Grandma Jackson arrived, wearing a little bunch of bells on her coat.

"Oh, my granddaughters!" She pulled Wen and Emily close to her.

The pile of gifts under the tree had grown. So many presents! Enough for each kid at the orphanage. Everybody took turns opening their gifts.

At dinner, Wen's father raised the mug Wen had given him. "Toast! A toast to all our family. To all those here at this table and to those far away, not able to join us today."

Wen felt a stab: Shu Ling wasn't here because Wen hadn't asked soon enough, when her father still had a job. And now Shu Ling was still at the orphanage, her leg getting colder and colder.

Wen's mother passed around heaping plates of roast beef, mashed potatoes, and string beans. Her father drank from his new coffee mug. Emily had propped her new stuffed bear against her plate, and her mother smelled especially strong of lemon.

*So much food*, Wen thought. *So many presents from under that tree.* Compared to the orphanage, her family had so much. Wen imagined Shu Ling licking the Christmas vinegar from her dumplings.

Would Shu Ling really be an extra, even now?

Wen tried to push the question away. But as the others chattered and ate around her, the question kept tugging inside her.

*You already know the answer,* Wen told herself. *Don't ask.*

But so little time was left before Shu Ling turned fourteen. Seventeen days.

While her mother served seconds, Wen felt her question ready to burst. She couldn't hold back any longer.

"Have something to ask whole family," Wen blurted.

"Go on, Wen." Her mother looked up, surprised.

"Know we cut out extras. Know Dad just working at the Regal place until he finds computer job. But—" Wen felt dizzy and her breathing came hard. "But," Wen persisted, "is it possible, our family can adopt Shu Ling?"

Wen waited. Nobody spoke. Nobody even ate.

"You . . ." Her mother faltered. "Wen, you want us to adopt Shu Ling?"

Her father and mother exchanged glances.

"Oh, Wen," her father said. "Money's so tight. We can't afford another child."

"Shu Ling sleep on my bed number two. She not eat much. Wear my clothes. Not take up much space. Maybe we have yard sale, make more monies for her," Wen said.

"It's not that, Wen. Until I get a job, we don't have an extra dime. We couldn't even afford the adoption fees or the flight to China right now."

Wen blinked away hot tears. "But we have big dinner, big tree, many presents."

"I know that compared to the orphanage, we seem really rich. But we just don't have a cushion, Wen," her mother said.

"Cushion," her father explained. "Extra money. We don't even have enough money to pay all of our bills on time."

"We know how much you love her, Wen. We really do. But we just can't afford it, do you understand?" her mother asked.

Wen gulped back her tears and felt them stuck in her throat.

"Cannot adopt Shu Ling," Wen said. She gazed around the table. Her father was wiping his forehead. Emily stirred her mashed potatoes. Her grandmother had her arm around the back of her mother's chair. Her mother was dabbing her eyes with a napkin.

Wen lowered her head and stared at her plate. Through her eyelashes, she saw Emily's little hand move her stuffed bear across the table and prop it against Wen's own glass of milk.

"Wen, are you OK, honey?" Her father rubbed her arm.

"OK," said Wen dully. "I know, no monies."

"You're bound to find Shu Ling a family any day now, sweetie," her mother soothed.

Grandma Jackson took off her stole. "Wen's chilled, Chris. Wen, darling, wear this."

Wen's mother stood up and wrapped the stole around Wen. Then, very briefly she put her arms around her. "We're so sorry, Wen."

Wen tried to force a smile, but her face stayed expressionless.

She was quiet for the rest of the meal. Her father tried to tell funny stories about Regal Electronics, and Grandma Jackson talked about the people at her retirement home. Emily told knock-knock jokes. But Wen felt their eyes stray toward her.

After Grandma Jackson went home that night, Wen and Emily threw away all the torn-up wrapping paper and vacuumed up all the pine needles around the tree. Wen's mother stacked up the gifts in neat piles, and her father cleaned the kitchen. Then Christmas was over.

When she finally slept, Wen dreamed she was racing through the dark orphanage, calling for Shu Ling. She tore to the common room, where Shu Ling might be eating noodles as she squatted on the cement floor. But Shu Ling wasn't there. Down the hall, Wen heard crying. She sped to the infant room and searched the cribs, but Shu Ling wasn't feeding the babies. She ran into the girls' bedroom, toward Shu Ling's cot.

Suddenly Director Feng towered over her.

"You are looking for Shen Shu Ling?" He leered. "She waited for you on the hill, for the news of her lucky day. But you broke your promise. There was no one here to take care of her leg. The skin turned black and Dr. Han had to amputate. But he was too late."

"Shu Ling!" Wen cried at Shu Ling's bed. Under the thin blanket, she could detect the stump that had been Shu Ling's leg. Wen knelt by Shu Ling's head and heard her breathing in short, shallow gasps, as if she were suffocating. Her lungs were giving out.

"Where is the family you promised me?" Shu Ling whispered.

"I'm so sorry." In tears, Wen tried to stroke Shu Ling's hair. But Shu Ling shrunk back, away from her. Wen put her head on Shu Ling's chest and heard her heart beat slower and slower. Wen took Shu Ling into her arms. For a moment, her eyes met Wen's.

"*Mei mei,*" she whispered.

Then she rolled back, heaving a final gasp.

And then Shu Ling died.

Wen woke herself up with a scream. Her sheets were drenched in sweat.

*Just a nightmare,* she told herself.

But when she thought of Shu Ling dying in the orphanage, her own breathing came in short gasps, as if she too were shutting down. Wen plunged into a deep darkness that no holiday light could pierce.

# twenty-three

Hey, how did Christmas go?

A text from Hannah! Using her thumbs the way Hannah had taught her, Wen picked out the letters to text back:

So much happened! How was seeing your father?

Wen waited until she heard a beep and then opened the "Hannah" envelope on her phone screen.

Ugh he left right after dinner even tho he said he was gonna stay longer and then said he might come back yesterday. Obviously he didn't. What happened with you?

Wen tapped a lot of wrong keys, had to press Clear, and finally hit the Send button.

I asked my family to adopt Shu Ling but they said no. Not enough money. I don't get it, we have a ton of food in our house. Except bacon.

Another beep.

> That stinks! Maybe they want to but they're
> scared things will get worse, especially with
> your dad not having a job.

Wen tapped back:

> He has job. Regal Electronics.

From Hannah:

> Maybe it's not enough. They should adopt her
> but I learned that sometimes parents know
> things, more is going on than you might think.
> Did they seem sorry tho?

Wen texted back.

> Yeah they all felt bad. Tried to feed me
> chocolate.

Hannah replied:

> Still stinks! How many days left?

Wen knew instantly.

2 weeks and 2 days.

Then a beep.

> Not much time. Gotta go to Maine now. Mom
> yelling at me. I'm sure someone will pick Shu
> Ling soon.

The next day, Wen switched between the different advocacy blogs, all urging people to choose Shu Ling. Why wasn't anybody adopting her? What was going wrong?

Wen picked up the phone. Maybe Nancy Lin would know what the problem was.

"Hello, Wen. Always such a pleasure to hear from you," Nancy said.

"Nancy, have big question," said Wen. "I do everything. I post with online group lookout people. I find her, I rewrite description, I add portrait. I contact all the stand-up people, Shu Ling on all the *ad-vo-ca-cy* blogs. So why nobody see her and say, that's our daughter? Why?"

"Oh, Wen. You've done everything right." Nancy sighed. "Don't give up yet."

"Not giving up," Wen said. "Just asking."

She could hear Nancy take a deep breath. "You've been an amazing advocate for your friend," Nancy said. "Unfortunately, there are thousands of waiting children, Wen. Thousands. And not as many families ready to adopt these children. A single child, especially one who's getting older, sometimes just doesn't get picked, no matter how nice she is."

*Thousands of kids.*

Wen half-listened as Nancy said in her hopeful voice there was plenty of time, not to get discouraged.

But all Wen heard was *thousands of kids,* and all she saw was the shrinking row of days remaining.

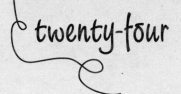

# twenty-four

"It snowed last night, Wennie!" Emily woke Wen by pouncing on her bed. Wen glanced outside the window. Ice-coated tree branches bent to the ground in graceful curves, like cranes' necks. Snowdrifts piled high as hills glittered in the sun.

"Have you ever seen so much snow before, Wennie?"

"Have big blizzards in China, sometimes make furnaces go out." Wen shivered, remembering Shu Ling and her leg.

"Not here. Too bad it's vacation. If it were during school, we would have had a Snow Day!" Emily told her.

"What is this Snow Day?" Wen asked.

"No school, Wennie. Come on, let's go sledding in the park." Emily got off Wen's bed. "Hurry up!"

From the hall closet, Emily pulled out two big plastic saucers, one pink and the other bright yellow.

"How go down hill on dishes?" Wen asked.

"Get dressed. I'll show you."

Wen eyed the computer in the kitchen. She had planned to e-mail Sandy, Tom, and the other bloggers. Thirteen days remained. Less than two weeks.

"Sorry. I cannot. Much to do this morning," said Wen.

"Do?" Emily repeated. "What's better than sledding, especially if you've never been, Wen?"

"On computer," Wen began.

"You're always on the computer!" Emily accused. "You never play with me! You never watch cartoons with me. You never read books with me. You just look for that girl on that stupid computer!"

Hands on her hips, Emily screamed, "Everybody was so excited about you, Wen! 'Oh good,' they said. 'Now you'll have a big sister.' But all you care about is that other sister of yours. She isn't even your real sister. I'm your real sister. But you don't act that way. You know something, Wen?" Emily glowered as she spat out her words. "I wish you never came here!"

She grabbed her pink sled and tore out of the house.

As if she'd been hit, Wen sunk and sat, paralyzed, on the other sled. Around her, the air seemed to vibrate with Emily's words, swirling like angry hornets around her.

Then Wen noticed Emily's parka lying on the floor. She'd been so mad, she'd left the house with no jacket. Emily would get too cold without it.

Wen zipped up her own coat, threw Emily's jacket over her arm, and jogged toward the park. Shading her eyes, she scanned the slope for Emily. Wen saw Michelle and Sophie, and a skinny boy with a shaved head from Wen's class who always got in trouble for thumb wrestling. But no Emily.

Then Wen spotted her, her little body shivering in jeans and a sweatshirt.

"Emily," Wen called, "you forgot your jacket!"

But Emily had already flung herself on her sled and didn't hear her.

Across from Wen, kids sped down the slope, snow scattering as they flew.

"Time for a train! Make a long line and hold tight onto the sled in front of you," yelled a boy Wen recognized from the bus stop.

Wen spied Emily and one of her friends piled on Emily's pink saucer, gripping the sled in front of them.

"Everyone push on the snow to get us started," ordered the boy at the head of the train.

"Go!" shouted another girl in Wen's class.

Wen stood to the side as the train picked up speed and flew down the hill. At the bottom, the sleds piled up in a heap.

Then Wen heard screaming.

"My leg, my leg!" Emily wailed. She lay writhing on the snow.

"Randy's metal sled smashed into it," some kid shouted.

"It's bleeding really bad," another kid said. "Gross."

The kids clustered around Emily.

"Move, please, that's my sister!" Wen screamed, pushing her way through the crowd to Emily, who was paler than the snow. Blood seeped out of cuts on her cheeks. Crouching over Emily, Wen took a clean tissue from her pocket and pressed the tissue over Emily's gashes, just the way she had stopped the toddlers' bleeding shins and knees at the orphanage.

"Emily, we get you home right away. You can stand up?"

"I don't know, Wennie," Emily cried.

"OK, I get you up very slowly. Then you rest your arm on me." With both hands, Wen pulled Emily up, then let her lean on her arm as they walked home, *stomp-drag, stomp-drag.*

Back home, Wen and Emily found their father in the kitchen.

"God, what happened?" he asked. "Is she OK, Wen? Should we call 911?"

"Just cuts, Dad. I stopped the bleeding but we clean them now."

"I got wounded, Daddy!" Emily exclaimed. "Blood gushed out all over the place. And Wennie rescued me." Eyes sparkling, she squeezed Wen's hand. "She barged through all the kids and she said, 'That's my sister.' Just like that."

Wen grinned. She led Emily to her bedroom, where she and her dad cleaned Emily's cuts. Wen helped Emily take off her wet clothes and dried her with a towel. After that, she bundled Emily into her PJs and tucked her into bed.

Then, bending over, Wen kissed Emily on the forehead. In her ear, she spoke softly.

"Rest now, *mei mei*," she said.

# twenty-five

"Any news on a family?" Hannah asked Wen at the bus stop, the morning school started after winter break. They hadn't even had a chance to say hello yet.

"Nothing," Wen said. "Tomorrow, just one week left."

"Terrible. Not much time," Hannah murmured as they boarded the bus.

"Your dad call?" Wen settled herself beside Hannah.

"Nope." Hannah tried to shrug, but just slumped against the seat instead.

"Not right. He should call you. Every day, even," Wen stated.

"Stinks," Hannah said.

"Stinks greatly," Wen agreed.

Sharing iPod earbuds, Wen and Hannah stared out the window at the sooty, drab snowbanks all the way to school.

Once school had started, Ms. Beckwith led them to the computer lab, where they were supposed to write something about what they did over vacation.

"Psssst," Hannah whispered to Wen. "Let's open up Shu Ling's Web site."

Wen knew this was against computer lab rules. You weren't supposed to go online unless it was part of the assignment and the teacher gave you specific Web sites. But just a quick peek at Shu Ling, really fast, how bad was that?

"Hurry!" said Wen. She typed in the Worldwide Adoptions URL and Shu Ling sprang onto the screen.

"Michelle, Sophie, check this out, quick," Hannah said, keeping her voice soft.

Michelle and Sophie peered at Wen's computer.

"Who's she?" Michelle demanded.

"My friend in China. Needs family. So I put her on Web site," said Wen.

"Wow!" Sophie said. "You did that yourself? That's really amazing."

"What's up with the 'Eight Days Left'?" Michelle asked.

"After eight days, my friend too old to be adopted. Nobody pick her, she stays in China." Wen hesitated. Suppose Michelle made fun of her?

She glanced at Hannah, who was watching Michelle uneasily.

"She stays in China for good?" Michelle asked.

Wen tensed her shoulders and nodded. "For good."

Michelle gazed at Shu Ling's photo. "So she was your best friend over there? And now you kind of miss her?" She eyed Hannah.

"Miss her greatly," said Wen.

"I get it now." Her voice low, Michelle looked straight at Wen. "I really hope she finds a family."

"Thanks, Michelle," Wen said.

"Hey, here comes Ms. Beckwith," Sophie warned.

As Wen shut down the Web site, Michelle smiled at her for the first time.

And Wen gave her best half-moon smile back.

After school, Wen clicked on Worldwide Adoptions for another glimpse of Shu Ling.

Her photo was gone!

Was her birthday even earlier than her file had said? Had she already turned fourteen and they'd sent her file back to the orphanage?

Wen called Jenny Peters right away. "Where's Shu Ling?" Wen asked.

"Let me find out," said Jenny Peters.

Wen felt dizzy, like she might faint.

"It says here that a family has locked Shu Ling's file for seventy-two hours."

"What is this locked?" Something important had happened and Wen didn't understand.

"They have seventy-two hours to consider Shu Ling, have a doctor go over her medical records, and then decide if they'll adopt her."

"They might pick Shu Ling?" Wen repeated. Could this be possible?

"Yes. It's great news, Wen!" Jenny said. "They're a wonderful family. And I have to say, they called me three or four times, ever since they read what you wrote about Shu Ling. It was the way you described her, Wen, that convinced them to consider her. You should feel really proud."

Wen felt her chest expand. "Thank you," she said. "Where this family live?"

"They've got three adopted children from China and they live in Florida."

"I talk to them, maybe? Tell them more about how Shu Ling make nice daughter?" Wen suggested.

"No. That would go against agency policy. But don't worry, I'll call you as soon as I know."

Wen hung up the phone.

"Hey!" Wen shrieked so loud for her mother, her own ears tingled. "Shu Ling might have a family! Almost. Seventy-two hours. Family is thinking about adopting Shu Ling!"

"That's wonderful!" her mother said, coming into the room.

"Then she live in Florida village," said Wen. "Where is this Florida? We can visit?"

"Florida isn't that close. But we could use credit card miles or something. We'll find a way, Wen."

"What is it like, the Florida place?" Wen asked.

"Florida? Well, right now, Florida is hot. While we're freezing up here in the north, Florida is very, very hot! And the trees have long leaves on them. Palm trees."

Her mother waved her arms in the air, like branches swaying.

Wen closed her eyes and envisioned herself sitting beside Shu Ling in the hot sun of Florida with leafy trees behind them.

*It's so hot*, mei mei, Shu Ling would say. She would have pinned her thick braid around her head to keep her neck cool.

*Way too hot*, Wen would agree, fanning herself with her hand.

They would grin at each other, not minding the heat one bit.

After dinner, Wen and her family lined up their chairs by the computer and waited for Shu Ling's photo to reappear on the Worldwide Adoptions Web site.

"You're sure this will tell us something, Wen?" her father asked.

"Jenny Peters say as soon as family pick Shu Ling, picture go back on Web site with big golden flag, say 'Matched with Family.'"

"I'm getting bored," Emily whined. "Nothing's happening. Can I go play?"

"Sure, sweetie," said their mother.

"Keep me posted." Wen's father got up too. "I've got to study some for my interview tomorrow."

"Interview of the telephone?" Wen asked.

"No. Second, real-live interview." Her father beamed a little. "Call me if you see anything."

Wen and her mother sat side by side at the computer, staring at the other children on the Worldwide Web site.

"Little bit like watching a movie," said Wen. "But maybe nothing happen for a while. Maybe not for another two days!"

"How about we come back in half an hour?" her mother suggested.

At seven thirty, still no photo of Shu Ling had appeared. Wen reached for her cell phone.

> Hi Hannah, Shu Ling might have family! Family
> is thinking about it. Photo go off Web site until
> family decides. Check to see if photo come
> back, Matched with Family flag across bottom,
> for good news.

At eight thirty, still no Shu Ling. Wen's phone beeped.

> Awesome, Shu Ling might have a family! I'm

on her site too. No photo yet but I bet it's
coming! :-)

Finally, toward eleven o'clock when still no photo had
appeared, Wen and her mother turned off the computer,
and Wen went to bed.

The next morning, Wen opened up the Worldwide
Adoptions site. Shu Ling's photo was still gone.

"Mom made me turn off my computer around nine last
night. Any Shu Ling with flag yet?" Hannah asked Wen as
they walked into their classroom together.

"The family still thinking," Wen mumbled. She was so
tired, she could hardly talk.

"What's happening with your friend?" Michelle looked
up from putting on her lip gloss before class started.

"Nothing yet," Wen said.

The next day, with twenty-four of the seventy-two hours
remaining, Wen opened the computer, her fingers heavy
with dread. And there, at the top left, was Shu Ling's face.
Below her picture, Wen saw a bright yellow banner, drawn
with ripples, as if it were waving in some sort of procession.
The flag proclaimed "Matched with Family!"

"Hey! Everybody! Whole family!" Wen screamed.
"Come quick!" She jumped up and down.

Her mother came running downstairs, Emily raced in, and her father strode in from his office. They all gathered around Wen at the computer.

"Matched with Family! Whooo-eee!" Emily hooted.

Her father put his arm around Wen and gave her a thumbs-up sign.

"Oh, Wen, I'm so glad," her mother said.

The Matched with Family banner seemed to Wen to be streaming right in their kitchen. Suddenly Wen felt so light, she thought she might float off the floor and fly, just like that banner.

Shu Ling had a family at last!

# twenty-six

On Saturday Wen clicked the Worldwide Adoptions Web site to rejoice once more at the bright yellow Matched with Family flag under Shu Ling's photo.

But when the page finally opened, Wen gasped.

Shu Ling's photo was gone again!

What had happened? Shu Ling wouldn't be taken off the Web site just because she was matched. Once a waiting child got matched, Wen knew Worldwide Adoptions left that picture with the banner flying on their Web site for a long time, so people could feel glad that some kid had been picked by a nice family, happy ending.

The advocacy blogs went crazy when a kid got a family. "Children Who Wait" put the words "Joined a Family," flashing like a traffic light. "Take Me Home" had a whole section called, "Guess Who Found a Family?" with rows of beaming children, all chosen.

Wen reached for her phone to call Jenny Peters and then remembered it was the weekend.

The missing photo could mean only one thing. Shu Ling's new family had given her back, before they even met her. Wen's words hadn't been completely convincing after all.

There weren't enough days left. Who would pick Shu Ling in the next four days? Shu Ling's chance for a family was gone for good.

Wen rested her head against the computer monitor and began to sob.

Her mother came to her side. "Wen, what is it?"

"Shu Ling gone." Wen felt waves of sadness gather inside her, churning. If she didn't do something, she would explode.

"Oh no!" her mother wailed. "What happened? Maybe it's just a mistake, sweetie."

"Think family changed its mind." Wen blinked hard.

"We don't know, Wen. Jenny Peters can tell us on Monday." Her mother stroked Wen's hand.

"Hey." Wen couldn't sit any longer. "I go on short bike ride. Very short."

"A bike ride?" her mother asked. "Wen, you're very upset. Shouldn't you wait a while?"

"Need to do something, not stand around," Wen said. "I come back. I promise."

Wen zipped up her parka and hopped on her bike. She pedaled hard, as if to push down the blank photo space and all the losing. The houses whizzed by her as she pumped, her chest straining. Her lungs began to make short, throaty rasps.

She imagined Shu Ling, waiting for a family that had already given her back before they even met her. She saw Shu Ling without hope, limping off to the hill, lost for good.

Finally, when her legs ached too much to pedal, Wen steered for home. She left her bike by the garage and clung to the porch railing. Wen began to gag. She bolted into the bathroom, crouched over the toilet, and threw up. Just when she thought she was done, she retched and threw up again.

Wen's mother pulled open the door and raised her from the cold tiles.

"Come." She guided Wen to her bed and tucked a comforter around her.

Wen's mother sat beside her. "I am so sorry about Shu Ling."

"I sorry too," Wen said.

They didn't speak anymore because there was nothing else to say.

That afternoon, after Wen had slept, Hannah came over with her jewelry kit.

As she led Hannah to her room, all Wen could think about was her promise to Shu Ling, broken forever, like a shattered water jug.

"Wen, what's up?" Hannah asked. "What's wrong?"

"Shu Ling's family changed their mind. Gave her back," Wen told her. "Her photo fly off Web site."

"No 'Matched with Family' anymore?" Hannah asked. "Oh, Wen!"

Wen could only nod.

"It really stinks, Wen," Hannah said.

Wen wanted to say, *Yes it does, and how will I go on?* But she was so empty inside, no words came.

"I guess you don't want to talk about it, right?" Hannah asked.

"I cannot."

"OK, then." Hannah settled herself on Wen's bed and spread out her plastic boxes of beads. "You like the shiny ones best, right?"

Wen nodded absently. *You broke your promise,* she admonished herself.

Wen gathered the sparkly beads in her lap. Only now the sparkle was gone and the beads were just little balls of cheap colored glass.

After half an hour of silence, Hannah said, "Well, it's not like you asked but just so you know, I spent the day with my father yesterday."

"Oh." Wen had only half heard Hannah. She was far away, missing Shu Ling. The ache had set in so deeply, she now felt bone pain.

"I have things going on in my life too," Hannah said.

"You could say, 'Oh, how was it with your dad?' Something like that. Even if you had your own stuff to deal with."

Wen raised her eyes from the beads to gaze at Hannah. "Sorry, Hannah. How was it with your dad?"

"Bad. He has a new girlfriend and I hate her." Hannah stopped stringing beads.

"You met her?" Wen asked. "Yesterday?"

"Yeah. She took us out to dinner. She and my dad were holding hands the whole time. It made me sick!" Hannah blurted.

"They should not have held hands, not with you there. And your father should not be with this weird new lady," Wen said.

"I couldn't stand it," Hannah said as she jiggled the beads in the palm of her hand. "I get so mad!"

"It's not fair," Wen said, rubbing Hannah's back.

"Thanks. Here, Wen, I made you a surprise." From her tote, Hannah handed Wen a box. Wen opened it and pulled out a crystal beaded chain. Dangling from the chain was a half-heart charm, jagged on one edge. Across the shiny surface, Wen read the word "Special."

"It's a friendship necklace," Hannah explained. "I made the chain with those tiny beads, and I picked out the charms myself. See, I have a necklace too, with the other half of the heart, with the word 'Friends.' Your half fits into mine. So when we put them together"—she took her necklace from her neck and placed it beside the half in Wen's palm—"the words say 'Special Friends.'"

Wen stared at the joined hearts nestling in her hand.

"Because that's what we are, right?" Hannah asked. "Special Friends."

Wen paused. Nobody could ever replace Shu Ling, not even Hannah. She'd broken her promise to Shu Ling. How could she just turn around and become special friends with somebody else?

Briefly she admired the necklaces, intertwined, and brushed the engraving with her fingertips.

"What's wrong? Don't you want to be special friends, Wen?" asked Hannah, her voice wavering.

"Of course." Wen forced a small, tentative smile.

"But you're not sure. I can tell. And all along I thought we were getting to be such good friends."

Wen saw that Hannah was blinking hard.

"Beautiful necklace, Hannah," she said.

"But you'll never wear it. You don't want to." Hannah scooped all the beads back into their boxes. Her hands were trembling. "I have to go, Wen." This time Hannah didn't hug her.

Wen held the half-heart necklace in her hand and watched Hannah leave.

# twenty-seven

"Hey, what you doing?" Wen asked when she came down-stairs on Sunday and saw her mother at the computer, eyes fixed on the blank square where Shu Ling's photo used to be. "Just sitting there?" Wen noticed her mother was hold-ing a tissue, as if she'd been crying.

"I was just peeking." Her mother moved to make space for Wen. "I got to thinking maybe they just took her pic-ture off for repairs or something."

Wen gazed at her mother, her blue eyes now red-rimmed and swollen. *She knows,* Wen thought. *She really gets how much I love Shu Ling.*

Her mother understood because Wen had talked to her about Shu Ling. Wen was certain that if people just knew Shu Ling like she did, they would love Shu Ling too. Maybe she had to talk to people face-to-face, so they could really hear what made Shu Ling so special. She could go door to door, like Halloween. She even had a stack of leftover fly-ers in her room.

Then Wen reminded herself about what had happened after she'd gone to McDonald's last fall. Her parents warned her never to go off like that again.

"Hey," Wen said, "I go on little walk, give out more flyers."

"What?" Her mother pushed her glasses onto her head.

"Door to door, like Halloween," said Wen. "Tell people about Shu Ling myself."

Wen's mother sighed. "Oh, honey, I know you're trying everything, but do you really think—" She paused, then said gently, "Besides, Wen, Shu Ling is off the Web site altogether."

"Have to do everything possible," Wen nearly begged. "Maybe Jenny took photo off because no more time left, but if person call Jenny and ask about Shu Ling, would still be possible."

"Today's Sunday. Can you do it tomorrow, after school? You seem so tired today, Wen, and you haven't eaten a thing."

"After today, only two days left." Wen gestured toward the calendar.

"Well, OK. If it will make you feel better, go ahead, Wen. But just around the block, do you understand? Stay nearby."

Wen nodded as she stuffed some flyers into her parka.

"Remember this," her mother called, holding up Wen's phone. "It gets dark early in January, Wen. Don't be gone long."

"I come back soon."

Wen walked around the block, ringing doorbells. But nobody was home. She crossed the street. Soon she noticed the buildings had changed from low brick houses to taller ones. She stopped in front of a brown house surrounded by leafless shrubs. Thick curtains covered all the windows.

Wen wanted to go back. She couldn't ring the doorbells of these big houses where strangers lived. Then she thought of Shu Ling, chilled in her bed, as she waited for Auntie Lan Lan to say, "It's your lucky day; Wen has found you a family."

Wen strode up the walk and pushed a button, just the way she and the others had done on Halloween. She heard a chime inside. Wen shifted her weight and rehearsed her line. Suppose when she opened her mouth, she couldn't remember any English?

"Yes?" A tall man in a jogging suit towered over her.

"I—" Wen stammered. Her mouth had gone so dry she couldn't move her tongue.

"Sorry, not today. We give to so many causes already." The man kept his hand on the doorknob.

"This is not about money." Her fingers shaking, Wen fumbled with the flyer.

But he'd already shut the door.

She'd been too slow. She hadn't talked quick enough. She should have said, "Do you want to adopt a nice girl?" fast, before the person closed the door. She'd do better at the next stop. Wen strode to a house as big as a castle. She pushed a pearl button, which she decided must be the doorbell.

"Yes?" said a woman wearing a fuzzy brown sweater. She appraised Wen. "We signed the global-warming paper yesterday."

"This not—" Wen began. She extended the flyer to the woman carefully, as if she were giving her a precious document. "My friend, Shu Ling. She needs—"

The woman studied the sketch. "So you don't want money, you want us to adopt this girl?" The woman's voice was gentle now.

"She's a very nice girl," Wen stammered. Telling an unknown person about Shu Ling was harder than she thought. Taking a deep breath, Wen tried again. "You like her for your daughter?"

The lady pushed her glasses up her nose to see Wen better and told her that all her children were grown and she couldn't adopt Shu Ling, but maybe somebody else would. Then she gave Wen a peppermint and wished her luck.

At the next house, a boy about her own age answered her knock.

"Hi," he said. Behind him a little girl dragged a frayed blanket.

Wen waved a flyer near the boy. "My friend. She needs a family," she said.

"That's cool. I'll go ask my mom," the boy said. "I think she wants another kid." The little girl pattered after him.

While she waited, Wen peeked at the kitchen, its table set with four places. This was the greatest family. The boy was nice, and there was a little girl for Shu Ling to take care of. The house was near hers, so she and Shu Ling would go to the same school, probably be in the same class. After school they'd visit each other's houses and do their homework together, maybe stay for dinner.

"Sorry," said the boy, coming back. "My mom says no. Besides, she says she only wants real kids."

"Real kids?" Wen glared at him. "Shu Ling is real."

"Her *own*," said the boy. "Not adopted."

How could the lady think Shu Ling wasn't real? Shu Ling was as real as the boy standing in front of her. The only difference was, the boy had a family and Shu Ling didn't. Wen scowled at the boy and left.

Wen started up the street to try another house. Suddenly, she was very cold and very tired. Her feet hurt so badly she couldn't walk much farther.

She could ring another doorbell but she already knew. Nobody was interested. Wen put her flyers back in her jacket. She tried to retrace her steps, but the houses all looked the same. All she wanted to do was get back home. Her house was probably just around the corner.

But it wasn't. The houses began to blend in front of her. The sun had begun to set, casting shadows on the well-cut lawns.

Then Wen knew she was lost. She pulled out her cell phone and saw that it wasn't charged. Her legs weak, she sat down on the curb. As the sun slipped behind the tall houses, Wen shivered so hard, her teeth chattered.

Sitting on the curb in a neighborhood she didn't know, Wen began to cry. From long ago, she already knew.

No one would come for her.

Her mother probably hadn't asked herself, Where is Wen? She probably hadn't even noticed she was gone. She and the rest of the family had just had dinner and done the chores, not even missing her.

Or maybe she'd been away so long, her mother was mad. That was it. Her mother had said to just go around the block, but nobody answered at those houses. She shouldn't have crossed the street. Instead, she should have come right home, like she'd promised.

Her parents must be so mad they'd decided to leave her here, all alone in the dark.

It turned out she was an extra after all.

In the darkness, the trees towered like dragons. Wen pulled her jacket tighter and sobbed.

Somewhere, deep inside her, a little girl at a gate called out, "Mama!"

Overhead, the moon slid behind the clouds. In the darkness, Wen felt her terror rise. She got up off the curb to look for her mother but the night was so dark, she couldn't see in front of her. She sat back down, her back hurting as if pressing against something dry and hard.

"Mama!" the five-year-old girl inside her called.

All that came back was silence.

Wen waited a long time. She heard the church down the street chime eleven, then twelve. She knew she had waited like this a long time ago.

$$\ell\ell$$

A dog howled.

A siren screamed.

She was all alone.

Then she heard a car approach and screech to a halt.

"There she is!"

It was her mother's voice. Wen saw the family car in front of her. Her mother tore out of the front seat and ran to her. Emily followed right behind.

Wen's mother crouched by her, on the curb.

At the sight of her mother, Wen began to shake uncontrollably.

"I am so sorry. I got lost," Wen said.

"I said around the block," her mother accused. "No more."

Wen gazed at her mother's blue eyes, flashing now, no longer soft. Then she heard her father slam the car door.

"Oooh, you're in trouble," Emily whispered. "Watch out!"

Her father strode over to the curb, gripping his car keys.

"Wen, we told you not to do this! You just disappeared on us!" he shouted.

"I not mean—" Wen started.

"Wen, we didn't know where you were!" her mother said, her voice scratchy and hoarse.

"I am sorry. I got lost. I didn't mean to," Wen pleaded.

"You did this once before!" her father yelled. "You broke our rules, Wen."

"Very sorry. Never do this again. Ever." Wen covered her face with her hands.

"Do you get how worried we are when we can't find you?" her mother demanded.

"My fault." Wen could feel her tears drip on her fingers.

Her mother uncurled her fingers and handed her a tissue.

"Never again, Wen," her father said.

"When I got lost, know it was my fault." Wen paused. "But—"

She felt the distant cold creep into her once more. The darkness towered over her again.

"But I got so scared. I thought you would not come."

"Of course we'd come, Wen," her father said.

"Thought you not notice I was gone, or maybe too mad," Wen said. "So left me here, alone."

Wen's mother took her face in her hands and stared into her eyes so intently that Wen wanted to turn away, but her mother wouldn't let her. "Listen to me," she said. "We will never leave you. We're family. No matter what happens, Wen. Do you understand?" Then she repeated very slowly. *"We will never leave you."*

And the little girl from long ago knew, at last, that this was true.

"I get this now, Mom." The word she'd wanted to say all those months burst from her lips, spontaneously, like a song. Her mother's eyes lit up and for a minute, she glowed.

Sitting on the curb, Wen took a glimpse at her father, still pale, gripping his car keys. She glanced at Emily, drowsy, in her PJs. She felt her mother's shoulder against hers.

"Something I must tell you." Wen looked at the curb, to avoid their gaze. Then she said it. "I love you."

She waited for the long silence from long ago.

She strained for the reply that would never come.

"We love you too, Wen." Her father sat on the curb, his arm around her. Emily wedged her little hands into hers. Beside her, her mother drew her close and embraced her. As Wen sank into her mother's arms, she felt as if she fit, as if she had belonged there all the time.

# twenty-eight

On the bus Monday, Wen noticed Hannah sitting in a different seat from their regular place on the bus.

"Sit with you?" Wen asked.

"If you want." Hannah moved over, not looking up.

Wen wedged herself in the seat, her boots on her backpack, where she'd hidden her cell phone so she could secretly call Jenny Peters about Shu Ling's missing photo.

"Hi." Wen touched Hannah's shoulder. "Want to say I'm sorry."

"It's OK, I understand." Hannah edged closer to the window.

They rode in silence.

"Greatly sorry." Wen tried again. "I missed you this weekend. Figured out much about my family, you too."

As if she couldn't resist, Hannah turned toward her. "So what did you figure out about me?"

"This weekend I realized I have much right here in America. I have my family, I have you."

"But you keep pushing me away, Wen. Why wouldn't you wear the necklace? I worked so hard on it and every bead I strung, I thought, 'Here's me and Wen going bike riding. Here's me and Wen trick-or-treating next Halloween. Here's me and Wen going to the first day of middle school together.' And then you wouldn't wear it!" Hannah bit her lip. "First my dad goes, right? And then Michelle doesn't get it, but you do. So I wanted to be your friend, and even when you acted weird and kept disappearing from me, I told myself you just needed time. I wanted to invite you to sleepovers and get manicures together but I told myself, 'No, wait, she still misses Shu Ling.' So finally, I give you the necklace, and you won't even wear it. I'd expect something like that from Michelle. But not you!"

"I'm so sorry, Hannah. I did not pay enough attention to you," Wen said.

"Wen, I understand about Shu Ling. I know she'll always be your best friend. That's why I picked a Special Friends charm, not a Best Friends charm. I thought that would make it easier for you. But you couldn't even wear that!"

"I changed my mind. Shu Ling is my friend. But you are too! Want to wear this necklace, now. This is still OK with you?"

From her pocket, Wen lifted the silver necklace with the word "Special" engraved across the half heart.

"Please, Hannah. I be better friend, I promise!" Wen said.

"OK, you win!" Hannah fished her half-heart necklace from her backpack and the girls hooked the chains over each other's necks. Leaning into each other, they fit the two halves together.

"Special Friends," Wen read. She slipped her elbow through Hannah's.

As Wen and Hannah rode to school, they glanced down from time to time at their necklaces, glistening against their jackets.

At recess, Wen ducked behind the big tree near the fence and sneaked her cell phone from her pocket. Wen knew the no-cell-phone rule at school and that she could get in trouble. But she didn't care. She had to reach Worldwide Adoptions.

"Jenny, where is Shu Ling's photo?" Wen asked as soon as Jenny Peters answered.

"Oh, Wen," Jenny sighed. "I was going to call you. Something, ah, rather unexpected has happened."

"Please tell me!" Wen said. "Family gave her back?"

"No. Shu Ling will only tell you. That's what she said to Director Feng."

"Something has happened?" Wen's voice rose, her panic overtaking her.

"That's just it, Wen. We don't know. Shu Ling has said she will talk to you about whatever it is, but not to anyone else."

"I call her right away," Wen answered.

"You have to call her tonight, Wen, or it's too late. Don't forget the time difference. If you call Shu Ling tomorrow, it will already be her birthday in China. She'll be fourteen and too old," Jenny said.

*Time difference!* Wen hadn't thought of that. Suppose the phone lines were down tonight because of a blizzard in China? Suppose Shu Ling was at her auntie training and couldn't talk? Then there would be no more time.

At six o'clock that evening, as soon as she knew Shu Ling would be awake in China, Wen took the landline phone off its cradle. She went into her bedroom and closed the door to talk to Shu Ling alone.

Auntie Lan Lan answered.

"Auntie Lan Lan, it's me, Wen."

"I'm so glad you called! Here, let me get her."

Wen waited, focusing on Shu Ling's portrait to calm herself. Then she heard the familiar *stomp-drag, stomp-drag* coming toward the phone.

"Wen, you called!" Shu Ling said.

"Shu Ling!" Wen hadn't heard her voice for so long. "What's going on?"

Wen heard a pause on the phone and could almost see Shu Ling take the shoelace from her hair and twist it in her hands, the way she did when she had something hard to say.

"Wen," Shu Ling whispered, "I cannot do it."

"What?" Wen reeled. "You mean, you got sick or something, so you can't come right now?"

"No." Shu Ling's voice wavered. "I'm so sorry, *mei mei*. I cannot come at all."

"But why, Shu Ling? What about our promise?"

"I tried to want to come. Please believe me," Shu Ling said. "But this is the place I know best. I'm too old to leave."

"What are you talking about?" Wen asked. "You're thirteen. That's not too old!"

"Maybe not for you, but you're younger and you're braver than I am. I don't think I could get used to a new life in America. I wanted to. I miss you so much, *mei mei*. I carry your letters around with me in my shirt and at nighttime, I sing lullabies to only myself and I long for you to be near me. Sometimes I feel I cannot go on without you."

Wen gazed at Shu Ling's portrait, tacked on her bulletin board, the two of them, arm in arm. "I miss you all the time, Shu Ling."

Wen thought of the spinning game, how she used to twirl so fast, depending on Shu Ling's face to anchor her. Now Shu Ling was saying she wasn't coming after all. Wen felt as if she had crumpled in the yellow dust, too weak and too empty inside to get up. She was losing her best friend for good.

"We said we'd be together always," Wen said. "We made a deal! I only left because we'd visit each other in America. I went to all that trouble to find you a family."

Wen thought of how she'd pored over the rows of photos, how she'd posted her search request with the lookout
people. She thought about how she'd tracked down Shu
Ling's picture on the Worldwide Adoptions Web site and
how she'd rewritten her description to make it better. After
that, with the help of the stand-up people, she'd gotten her
on all the advocacy blogs. And now, when she'd finally
found Shu Ling a family, Shu Ling didn't want to go.

"Oh, Wen, please don't be mad at me."

"How could I not be mad? I kept my promise and you're
breaking yours." As Wen spoke, she tasted bitterness, like
the water she and Shu Ling used to drink from rusty tin
cups.

"My leg, Wen." Shu Ling paused. "This family can't
really want me, not with my bad leg."

"Ah," Wen said. "Your leg." She peered again at the portrait, Shu Ling's twisted leg hidden by gently flowing flared
jeans.

Last year, when they'd been playing the choosing game,
Shu Ling had stopped all of a sudden and frowned at her
twisted leg, protruding from her nightgown. Her eyes half
shut, her cheeks flushed, Shu Ling began rubbing Barbie's
curved legs. When Wen asked what was wrong, Shu Ling
shrieked that she wanted two nice long legs, just like
Barbie, just like everybody else. Then Shu Ling yanked out
Barbie's right leg and hurled it down the ditch.

"Shu Ling!" Wen had yelled. She scrambled into the

gully, rocks cutting her legs, dust making her eyes sting. She spotted the Barbie leg wedged between a dented milk tin and a dead bird. She unhooked the Barbie leg and climbed back to the dust space, where she cleaned the leg with her shirt and popped it back onto the Barbie.

"You shouldn't have thrown the leg, Shu Ling!" Wen said. "We could have both gotten in a lot of trouble. And you know what that means. It means Director Feng bans us from adoption. You should have thought about that."

"*Mei mei*," Shu Ling said, "I'm so sorry." Shu Ling sat on the tires, her bad leg crooked and her head in her lap.

"You can never do that again!" Wen told Shu Ling.

When Wen stooped to help Shu Ling get up, Shu Ling clung to Wen and sobbed. "I thought you had stopped being my friend."

"Oh, Shu Ling," Wen had said. "I could never stop being your friend."

They had never talked about that day again.

Now Wen said, "So it's your leg! Shu Ling, when I wrote about you on the Web site, I told about your leg. So this family already knows! They're fine with it. They want you anyway!"

"Another thing," Shu Ling said. "You told me yourself, Wen, how you were scared, how they seemed like strangers. I wouldn't even know how to *be* in a family."

Wen remembered how afraid she'd been of her mother's first kisses, her pushing Emily away when she wanted to play. She remembered working so hard to be a good daughter and not get sent back. She hadn't known how to be in a family either.

"You're right, Shu Ling. I've been scared too," Wen said. "Really scared. But you have to let them love you. You just have to let them."

With one hand, she picked up the family portrait that her mother had framed and set on her bedside table. There they all were, standing in front of McDonald's. In the back, her parents wrapped their arms around Wen and Emily. Her mother had that glow in her eyes and her father was opening his mouth, like he was saying cheese, even though of course cheese was for eating, not for saying while taking pictures. Grinning wide, Emily was hanging on to Wen, and even Wen was smiling.

"I only know how to be on my own, *mei mei*," Shu Ling said.

"I know you think you can be on your own. I used to think so too. But it's better with a family."

"How is it better? Trips to McDonald's and the mall-palace?" Shu Ling asked. "I don't need these."

"No. Being with a family is better because if you get lost, they drive around in their car until they find you. If you feel sad, they try to cheer you up, even if they don't really know what's wrong. If you get sick, they sit by your bed and take care of you. And if things get hard, like maybe there's less money, they still love you no matter what, because they're your family. That's what's better."

"And you learned to do this? You're not scared?"

Wen thought, then replied. "Shu Ling, sometimes, but not so much anymore."

"It would be worse for me, *mei mei*."

"No." Wen's voice gathered force. "Your family will help you."

The phone went silent. Holding her breath, Wen waited.

"I'd have a real family, Wen?" Shu Ling said slowly.

"A family has chosen you, Shu Ling. It's that red-thread thing Auntie Lan Lan talks about."

"The invisible one that connects people?" Shu Ling asked.

"Yes. You belong with them, Shu Ling," Wen said. "It is your lucky day!"

Shu Ling said nothing. In the background, Wen heard the babies crying, an auntie calling out for extra help, and the kids getting lined up for chores.

Still, Shu Ling did not speak.

Wen studied the portrait, pacing back and forth, forcing herself to wait.

"OK." Shu Ling spoke with confidence. "I'm coming. I have a family of my own now, and I'm coming."

"You're really sure, Shu Ling?" Wen asked.

"Definitely. See you in the village of Florida, *mei mei*!"

After she hung up, Wen shrieked, "Mom! Dad! Emily! Shu Ling's coming after all!"

Her mother raced in so quickly that Wen figured she must have been waiting outside the door.

"Oh, Wen," her mother sighed. As they hugged, Wen felt her mother's moist cheeks against her own. Her father bounded into her room, carrying the mug she'd given him, and Emily bounced onto Wen's bed.

Wen flung her arms around all of them. She had a family and now, at last, Shu Ling did too.

# twenty-nine

The first day of summer vacation, Wen and her family boarded an airplane. Ever since her dad had found a new job in February, they'd been saving up enough money to go to Florida and greet Shu Ling. Jenny Peters had given them special permission to be there for the arrival. Now the day was finally here.

What would it be like, seeing Shu Ling after all these months? It had taken so long for all the paperwork to be finished, both in America and China. Wen could feel her heart beating faster under her tank top. Shu Ling would be so surprised to see her! Wen hadn't told her she was coming.

Wen and her family got off the plane at the Miami airport. Shu Ling's flight was supposed to land in half an hour. Wen's family was planning to meet Shu Ling and her family right outside security.

The McGuires stopped in front of a lit-up sign that showed all arrivals and departures.

"'Flight 2230, Gate 25A,'" Wen's father read. "Oh, wait a minute. Says the flight is delayed."

"Excuse me, mister." Wen stopped a man in a dark-blue

uniform, with a tiny airplane sewn on his pocket. "How late is Flight 2230?"

"It was delayed because of some storm activity over Chicago. I'd say it should arrive here in about an hour."

An hour? Wen couldn't wait much longer.

"Let's get some lunch." Wen's mother motioned to the restaurants nearby. "She'll be here soon, Wen."

At a café, the family squeezed into a small booth by the window.

"Burger, Wen?" Her father grinned.

"Soda refills are probably free," Emily chimed in.

"I'm not so hungry, right now," Wen said.

Just then, Wen's phone beeped. A text message had come, from Hannah.

**Hey, how's it going? See Shu Ling yet?**

Wen texted back:

**Plane late. Will let you know.**

Wen's mother rose from the booth. "Come on, let's get some fresh air."

Downstairs, they pushed through a set of glass doors and felt a hot breeze. Wen saw the trees her mother had been talking about, with long trunks and thin leaves like spikes, standing against a very blue sky.

"Let's go to the beach while we wait!" said Emily.

"That's tomorrow, Emily," her father reminded her.

"We should go back," Wen said. "Plane might be early."

Upstairs, they waited by the walkway to the lobby and main concourse, where Shu Ling and her family would pass once they got off the plane. Then a voice over a loudspeaker announced, "Flight 2230 has landed at Gate 25A." As passengers pushed through the entrance, Wen jumped to her feet. But none of them was Shu Ling.

*Shu Ling, where are you?* Wen craned her neck.

Then she saw her. Her hair pulled back, Shu Ling walked with her new mother, her new father, a teenage brother, and two little sisters.

"Shu Ling!" Wen screamed.

Shu Ling gazed at the crowd, confused. Then she saw Wen.

"*Mei mei!*" Shu Ling shrieked. Wen and Shu Ling fell into each other's arms.

"Oh, Shu Ling, you're finally here!" Wen stepped away to see Shu Ling's face, beaming as bright as the Lunar New Year lanterns.

"Oh, *mei mei*, you have grown so beautiful. You are so . . . American!"

"You look beautiful too. I recognize that tunic. It is one I sent you!" Wen echoed Shu Ling's Chinese. After all, they had always spoken Chinese together, and Shu Ling would have plenty of time to practice English.

"Auntie Lan Lan said, 'This is your lucky day,' and she took it from the common wardrobe for me."

"Your lucky day. Finally!" Wen beamed.

"Thanks to you, *mei mei*. You kept your promise."

"You have a big family," Wen observed. "Your mother's hair is not that red."

"Her eyes are so round. And she speaks Chinese weird," whispered Shu Ling.

"You get used to these things." Wen gazed at the little girl whose eyes brimmed with adoration for Shu Ling. "That little girl, your sister," Wen began. "She loves you already. You can call her *mei mei*. She'd like that."

"But you are my *mei mei*, Wen."

"You can have two *mei meis*," said Wen.

Wen glanced over her shoulder, where her family was watching. She introduced her parents and Emily to Shu Ling. Then, with her new parents on either side of her, Shu Ling said, in perfect English, "Please meet my new family."

Everybody shook hands. A crowd of passengers surged around them.

"Maybe it's time to leave," Wen said. "We're getting together with you at the beach tomorrow."

"The beach in the Florida village. You're coming too?" Shu Ling's eyes widened.

"My parents agreed. It'll be so hot," said Wen. "You'll have to tie your braid around your head; it will keep your neck cool."

"Good idea, *mei mei*," Shu Ling said.

Shu Ling's little sister tugged on Shu Ling's shirt.

"We should probably go now," said Wen.

"*Zai jian*." Shu Ling raised her right hand and stroked Wen's cheek.

Wen and Shu Ling hugged for a long time. Then Wen stepped away. Shu Ling returned to her mother. Her father stood on the other side while her sisters and brother gathered around her.

"*Zai jian*," Wen whispered. As Shu Ling left, Wen caught sight of her long braid. She smiled.

Shu Ling had tied back her hair with a single red thread.

Then Wen saw her mother, her father, and Emily standing beside the glass door.

"Come on, Wennie!" Emily yelled.

Wen turned and walked toward her own family, who were waiting for her.

# Acknowledgments

In writing this book, I was blessed with my own red thread sisters, my writers' group: Jacqueline Davies, Mary Atkinson, Sarah Lamstein, and Tracey Fern. These dear friends cheered me on when the writing got hard and shared my joy as I neared the finish. I couldn't have written this book without them.

It must have been a red thread itself that connected me to my extraordinary editor, Leila S. Sales, Associate Editor at Viking/Penguin. Leila believed in *Red Thread Sisters* from the beginning. Gifted as both an editor and a writer, she helped me shape my manuscript into a better, stronger book. I'm also indebted to Viking's Janet Pascal for her thoughtful input and to Kristin Machado for her exquisite cover design.

I honor my smart and feisty agent, Regina Brooks, President of Serendipity Literary Agency and also an author. How I loved the way she championed *Red Thread Sisters*! And sharing a good laugh with Regina always lifted my spirits.

I'm grateful to Mary House, of Children's Hope International, who first gave me the idea for my book, while we ate at a tiny noodle shop in Wuhan, China. We'd just returned with our children from visiting their former orphanages. Mary told me, so poignantly, about her son's reunion with the friend he'd left behind. Her story stirred me.

I also thank Donna Medin, my neighbor, who welcomed me home from Wuhan and introduced me to the older daughter she had recently adopted from China. When I wanted learn more about these older children, Donna tirelessly posted my surveys on all her Chinese adoption listservs.

A heartfelt *xie xie* to my close friend Linda Lin, former director of the China program at Wide Horizons for Children, who helped us adopt our own two daughters from China some twenty years ago. The day I told Linda about my new story, she grasped both my hands. "You must write this important book," she urged. Over many cups of green tea, Linda described her work with the poorest Chinese orphanages and encouraged me to keep writing.

I cherish a circle of adoptive parents, most of whom had adopted one or more older children, who became both my experts and my friends. Dr. Jane Liedke, founder and former Executive Director of Our Chinese Daughters Foundation, Inc., answered my endless emails, and let me interview her at conferences, on a bus in China, and in her own home. She was part of my team, which included Suzanne Damstedt, Nutrition and Orphanage Assistance Director of Love Without Boundaries, as well as Sandra Allen, Marie Carmenati, Mary Faucher, Annie Hamlin, Donna Hartford, Jeanne Park, Jennifer Parker, and Longlan Cai Qilong. These were the women I turned to time and time again, with additional questions and frantic email requests for even more specific information. They offered me their experiences, their blogs, their photos, their videos— and themselves. Sometimes we laughed and sometimes we cried over the memories they imparted. To this circle of women, I extend my deepest gratitude and affection.

Special praise goes to two teenagers, Arden Allen and Jamie Hartford, adopted from China when they were older, who told me their own personal stories for *Red Thread Sisters*. Their openness took great courage and made my story a truer one.

I thank Amy Eldridge, Executive Director of Love Without Boundaries, for her astute observations about older child adoptions. I will donate a portion of *Red Thread Sisters*' proceeds to the good work Love Without Boundaries is doing.

I also appreciate the ongoing support of Shanti Fry, former president of Families with Children from China—New England, and Susan Avery, who posted my surveys to the entire FCCNE membership.

The adoptive parents of older children who filled out my four surveys supplied the background material I included in *Red Thread Sisters*. I am beholden to Abby Alias, Dianne Applegren, Eve Berne, Amy Brilliandt, Shari Butts, Andrianna Cassani, Pat Chatwick, Ann Chechile, Meg Clark, Martha Covington, Yvette Crabtree, Nancy Delpha, Karen Detweiler, Pat Gillule, Monica Hagewood, Karen Hawes, Betsy Hewitt, Starla Kull, Diane B. Kunz, Nancy Letson, Ellen Melchior, Clarissa Minocci, Maura Moran, Mary Morris, Joy Nobilini, Stacie Page, Kathy Pimloff, Donna Quinn, Valerie Rockwell, Robbin Rossi, Cindy Schutz, Laura Sullivan, Maeve Van Hoorde, Karen Ward, Sarah Wedaman, and Betsy Young. These parents took time from their busy schedules to provide, in vivid detail, their own powerful experiences of adopting an older child.

In writing *Red Thread Sisters*, I also valued guidance from several accomplished authors. Carolyn Coman was the "midwife" to *Red Thread Sisters*. I treasured Carolyn's talent, patience, and warmth, as she helped me mold my earliest drafts. Both a mentor and a friend, Carolyn followed my book's progress from its initial versions to publication. Additional critiques from Ellen Lesser, Kathy Appelt, Kara LeReau, Louise Hawes, and Xi Xi lit my way, like lunar lanterns.

And then there is my family. I wrap my arms around them and hold them close. I am forever grateful to my devoted husband, Tom Gagen, and my children, Jonathan, Elizabeth, and Katherine. My family sustained me during those years of research and revision. They tolerated my long absences in my attic where I was writing, and ate many a frozen meal so I could find more time to work.

And of course, thanks to my black Lab, Pepper, who slept at my feet as I wrote the book made possible by the generosity of so many others.

*Carol Antoinette Peacock*
NEWTON, MASSACHUSETTS
APRIL 2012

IF YOU WANT TO HELP ORPHANS IN CHINA who are still
waiting for families, or children in other international orphanages, you
can visit the Web sites of these organizations, which offer ways to take
action:

## Love Without Boundaries
http://www.lovewithoutboundaries.com/ Helps Chinese orphans
through their programs in education, foster care, healing homes, nutrition, orphanage assistance, and a sponsorship program that enables
donors to sponsor a child.

## Half the Sky
http://www.halfthesky.org/en Dedicated to improving the quality of
care in Chinese orphanages. Through a sponsorship program, people
can sponsor a child, a teen, a family, or one sick infant or toddler.

## Children's Hope International
http://orphan.childrenshope.net Helps orphanages in China,
Ethiopia, India, and Vietnam through programs in education, nutrition,
medical care, and family preservation.

## Holt International
http://www.holtinternational.org/ Aids orphanages in Cambodia,
China, Ethiopia, Haiti, India, Mongolia, Nepal, the Philippines, South
Korea, Thailand, and Vietnam. Sponsorship program provides medical care, education, childcare supplies, and family support to needy
orphans.